Spawn

Of

Dyscrasia

S.E. LINDBERG

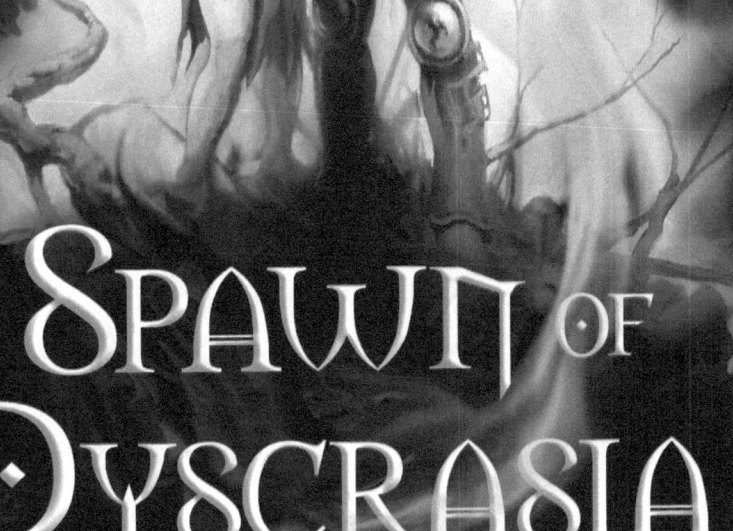

SPAWN OF
DYSCRASIA

Spawn of Dyscrasia
Copyright © 2014 by S. E. Lindberg
ISBN-10:0983826234
ISBN-13:978-0-9838262-3-1

Dyscrasia Fiction™ is a trademark of IGNIS Publishing LLC

IGNIS Publishing LLC
8064 Seabury Court, West Chester, OH 45069

The Morpheus Font is used with permission from Kiwi Media.

Front Cover Art © 2013 Ken Kelly
Back Cover Art and Map © 2014 S. E. Lindberg
Cover Design by S. E. Lindberg and H. L. Lindberg
Edited by Forrest Aguirre

·Dedication

Undying thanks to Team Lindberg:

Art Director, Heidi

Resident Mythologist, Erin

Truth Teller, Connor

Therapists, Shorty & Sweetie

Map

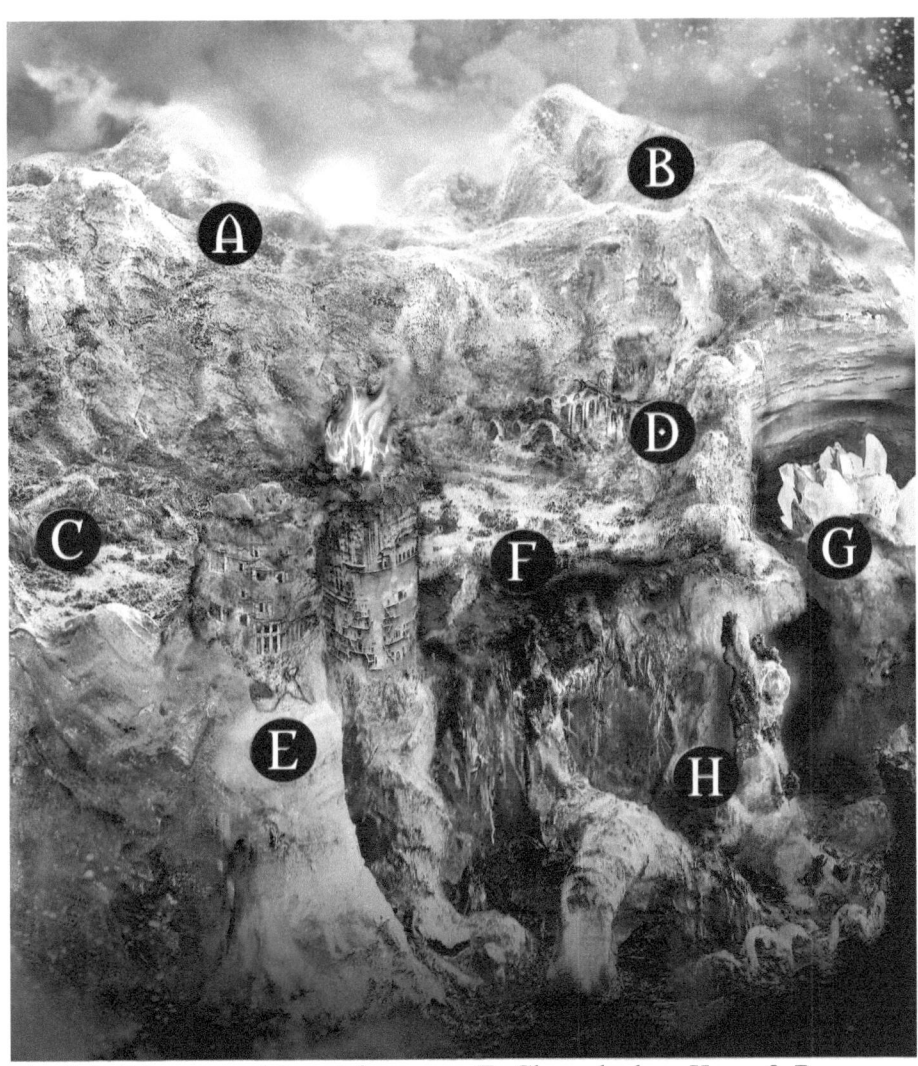

A: Calx Limestone Mountains

B: Arenite Sandstone Range

C: Haunted Gallwomb

D: Tonn Ghost City

E: Chromlechon Keep & Pyre

F: Blood Bogs & Gray Orchard

G: Hearth Tomb & Tonn Mines

H: Underworld Hollow

Contents

I: A Standard Bearer Leaves the Keep

H ELEN DID NOT fit in.
          She knew.

She trailed the other neophyte curators, shuffling through the tunnels. The golem, Doctor Grave, was assembling them for a sudden, unrehearsed ceremony. Although the Doctor governed the Chromlechon Keep, he was not its ultimate leader. He answered to two Gray Lords, the more reclusive of which was losing its healer and required a replacement. He led the parade of candidates to the amphitheater.

It was a solemn time, especially for Helen. A former acquaintance lay dying in the chamber ahead, and she mourned for her already. Distracted by thoughts of death, she had forgotten to fetch her banner. Irresponsible, she knew. Many rites required using it. Too late now. Maybe no one would notice. Better march forward ill-prepared than fetch it and be late. The other initiates proceeded in full regalia, and their unmarked flags swayed from staffs in front of Helen. Admittedly, they were more prepared for any ceremony than she was, but the occasion did not deter them from gossiping. They were less concerned about paying respects to the failing curator and more concerned about being selected to serve the lesser of the two Grays. They did not want to be here, but they would never question or delay the customs within the Keep. Helen found their chatter disrespectful:

"I wonder what she did to be sentenced to serve Lord Echo—"

"His next will become cursed like her—"

"Is her body contagious?"

"What was her name, anyway?"

The healer's name was Sharon, Helen reflected as she fiddled with a silk ribbon to secure a braid. She would never forget receiving the tie. Even though Sharon had been Echo's curer for as long as anyone could remember, and therefore isolated from the Keepers, the two had experienced the end of the Ill Age together. One never forgets the moment parents die.

Twenty years ago, Helen and Sharon were little girls. Sharon hailed from Clan Qual and often accompanied her parents to the highlands to purchase pelts from Helen's family. She always hid behind her mother, caring for a rag doll. She was detectable regardless, since her hair was a luminous skein of orange curls. The sun's rays seemed to get trapped within those curls, and grew more orange, as if enflamed. Sharon said little to nothing during these exchanges.

Sharon's doll was attractive. Its dress was a weave of shiny, silk ribbons. Its glass eyes looked wondrously glossy. If not for their miniature size, they appeared life-like. Crafting those marbles surely involved magic, Helen had thought, and so the doll must be magical too.

Helen's father, always encouraging adventures, wrapped Helen in a feline pelt and sent her and Sharon into the fields to play. Helen had been petite as a girl, and could enrobe herself entirely within the fur hood. Sharon followed, in awe of it. In Qual, all clothes had been hand-made, so Sharon could not conceive how the furry shawl was crafted. A cat and little doll chased each other, carefree in grass taller than they, until they heard a distant, urgent shouting.

I have not heard my father's voice since then. Helen was not sure if she felt sad or proud for surviving so independently. Her mother had always called her by her formal name: Helena. She recalled them yelling to her and Sharon, frantically begging them to come back to the safety of their home. A black storm laced with fiery threads rolled from the west. Before the girls could return, the sky abruptly collapsed, and the cabin was engulfed in a volcanic cloud.

Sharon and Helen awoke in the fields. They found themselves coated in ash. The skeleton of Helen's home smoldered. Playing in the fields had saved them from incineration. Parentless, they strayed together for days, roaming away from the devastation. Ignorance and exposure nearly killed them both. They would have died in the wilderness, had not magic intervened. A fairy cat, comprised of green embers, found them one night. The glowing parchment creature lured them south-west, toward the Keep. Who could deny such a divine calling?

They found beauty in wild flowers during their journey. These they picked. White lilies adorned Sharon's red hair; red poppies decorated Helen's white. To fix a braid from unraveling in Helen's hair, Sharon took a ribbon off her doll and knotted it. It remained two decades later, carefully moved upward every several months as her hair grew. Several dozen small relics, like beads and small metal rings, have since joined it. Abject charms inspired her. Helen evolved into a collector of sorts, ever appreciating the power of items others deemed spent. Most items did not fit in her hair. These she squirreled away under the Keep's crawlways in remote stashes.

Presently, she released her hands from the ribbon. She closed her azure eyes. Then she ran her fingernails against the flat hewn walls to ground herself in reality. She preferred the natural glossy surfaces of the lower strata than these carved walls gracing the tunnels nearer the surface. If she had ever to sacrifice a sense, it would be her hearing or sight. Taste or smell, perhaps. However, touch, above all, she would not relinquish. She would never give up the ability to feel.

She followed the others up the ramp toward the Operating Theater. It was time for them to adorn their flags in a ceremony. One would leave their apprenticeship under Doctor Grave, committing herself to official service. Helen had forgotten her flag, so she was going to have to improvise. As they funneled toward their seats, Helen broke from the line to sit apart. No one noticed her departure. They rarely sought her out anyway. Ironically, the others were dressed as if they wanted to participate. They all stood erect, wearing linen shifts overlaid with colorful waxen aprons and elbow-length gloves to protect their hands from toxic inks. Yet they did their best to look away: 'Look upon the sickly and sickly you become,' some said. It was no surprise that they did not look directly at the center stage either. Sharon lay there.

The Keepers had become accustomed to their present circumstances, putting aside the nightmares born from the cataclysm when the Gray Lords defeated dyscrasia. As the orphaned children of the Ill Age grew into adulthood, they created a new society of survivors within the Chromlechon Keep.

Helen was not inclined to conform. Her skin was ornamented with black splotches and splatters atop tattoos of cats, grasshoppers, and creatures from her daydreams. The darkness of these markings contrasted with the paleness of her skin and hair, which were oppositely-charged white. Her gaunt form belied her real age. Her boney shoulders slouched, and her collarbone hardly supported her ragged cat hide, which had been sized for a young girl, not a woman in her twenties. Her sacred pelt mantled her neck over the standard frock. She drew comfort in the memories continually seeping from it. A decade of wear had taken its toll. It resembled a mangled shawl now.

Helen turned her attention to the curator perishing at the center of the Theater. *Oh, Sharon, it is has been so long since we talked. I have missed you as you ventured. I wish you could hear me say 'farewell'.* Sharon had served as Lord Echo's lone inker for many years. None envied her, except Helen, perhaps, who deemed Sharon's role as more interesting than deficient. The Gray Foundling was less glorious and less attractive than Lord Lysis, who acted as king over the Keep. Conceived from a union of eldritch creatures and man, Echo was born with a monstrous litter in which all his siblings expressed various combinations of avian, insect, and human traits. Unlike his winged Gallwraith kin, Echo first appeared predominantly human. As he matured, the hybrid shed his fleshy, larval shell and assumed the shape of a colossal humanoid resembling a mantis. A set of wings were furled back and out of sight, and even if extended probably could not support his weight for a prolonged flight.

Now, his four legs and thorax were plated pearly white, which made the pale flesh of his torso appear dark, in comparison. His arms bent awkwardly, his dangling hands poised to lash. Impossibly large eyes, glossy black globes, stared down at his servant. As she died, the Gray Foundling and his Guard, whom she supported, grew weak. He was faint from lack of inking. His head drooped, and he leaned on his reanimated guardian, Bryhan.

Echo and Bryhan appeared darker than the lantern light of the Theater would seem to permit. He needed treatment. Helen knew that Echo's white blood merely hungered for power. His radiance would return to a white glow once satiated. After all, Doctor Grave had taught the Keepers the ways of alchemy and the history of the Lords' rising. Helen recalled his teachings, which had been given in this very place:

"There are two basic rules you must understand," the Doctor had professed from the Theater dais, his colossal cleaver in hand. "Two for now, anyway. The first is the Rule of Stone, which simply follows: hybrid blood always calcifies."

Masked in flayed skin, the Doctor wielded his blade and approached two hanging cages. The cabinets and display of tools were compulsively clean and organized. Residual fluids on tools tended to react violently with other liquids, so Grave's meticulous habits were warranted, lest the instruments be ruined. Rows of vials were banked on the shelves behind him, a stock he continually used and replenished. The glass jars held variegated chemicals both mineral and fluid, smoky and clear, sparkly and dull.

"When blood is stricken with dyscrasia, it has an imbalanced ratio of human and elder elements. This fluid is unstable and rapidly ossifies, especially upon contact with other diseased blood. Donations from our prisoners will illustrate the reaction." Grave slit the femoral artery of a vampyric harpy, its wings already clipped and body stuffed into an iron gibbet so compactly that its feathery legs protruded from the cage. The fresh carcass shivered as it released its blue blood, filling a bowl beneath it. Then the Doctor moved the bowl beneath the other prisoner and cut its legs. Soon a blood of lighter shade splashed into the bath of vibrant ichor. All in the theater were awed as the mixing of impure blood issued sparks. The liquid lost its blue color with each electric discharge, leaving the dish filled with a gray rock.

"However, when blood has the proper eucrasiac balance—as is within the blood of our Lords—it becomes a white amalgam: *lapis elixir*. Like the luminous molten rock that spits from mountain cores, *lapis elixir* is a liquid stone. It looks like cream, though it flows as slowly as mud. This ichor is thick and cool to the touch. Do not let its temperature fool your perception of its power. It contains more energy than the celestial stars." Then he ended the session. "Our lesson next month will describe the second principle: the Rule of Blood and Ether."

Helen would never forget that second demonstration either. The Doctor had walked the perimeter of the chamber extinguishing all torches save the one on center stage. Here he retrieved his cleaver and placed it on the operating table. Disrobing from his apron, the Doctor bared his chest. His flesh was gray clay. He was humanoid in form, but was not truly human. An earthen scar the width of Lysis' sword extended across his left breast. Silently, he turned the blade upright with his left hand and leaned forward. He did not flinch as the laceration opened anew. His flesh did not react as would human muscle, but split cleanly like fruit. He was known to be a golem, but, given his bipedal form and masked face, it was easy to overlook his inhumanity. Now his earthy composition was clear. Out from his flesh seeped *lapis elixir*, the white blood animating him.

The audience gasped.

"There are other rules, mind you, such as the Rule of Animation, which you will not master since possession is a skill beyond your purpose. Yet know this, the Lords reanimate we who would otherwise be lifeless." He stood upright and pulled the clay flesh open with both hands. The golem's homunculus heart was thus revealed, and its white ichor seeped out to bleed onto the torch. "Students, this blood is not properly mine."

Onto the final torch he directed his dripping wound. The fire struggled to breathe while being doused. Helen had thought it looked more like milk squeezed from a goat than it did fluid marble. "It belongs to Lord Lysis, who animates me."

The Keepers sat still awaiting for the Doctor to collapse.

"Now initiates. Ink your flags. Think upon the power of Lord Lysis and the beauty he inspires you to create."

All the neophytes, except for Helen, went to work. Within the hour, several dozen paintings were given form and color, only to have them drained of substance as the torch flared higher and higher. As was the case now, Helen had forgotten her flag then—a habit she was just beginning to exhibit. She remembered looking around in vain for a way to participate, but was unsuccessful, so she decided to act inconspicuous and wait the session out. The Doctor noticed her anyway. He stopped his rounds before her seat and stared at her with equal parts curiosity and incredulity. This ate away her esteem. In silence, Grave pointed to her arm, and walked off. He had prompted her to experiment. Apprehensively, she applied her inks to her arm. The marks faded instantaneously. It was then that Helen learned that flags were not necessary for magic to work. Any medium sufficed.

The group's creative energies had fed the *lapis elixir*, and it glowed brilliantly. Soon the entire Theater was brightly illuminated by the blazing white light of a single torch. And their canvases were blank again.

"You have rejuvenated your master's power and witnessed the Rule of Blood and Ether in practice," Doctor Grave said. "It follows: blood is the medium bridging the physical world with the ethereal, body to soul."

Grave had stood close to the lone fire. His mask cast a triangular shadow behind him. "Our Gray Lords animate their minions, cast spells, and perform sorcery by drawing on energy that is invisible to the living. It is the alchemical element called 'ether'. The Lords and we undead *see* it as flowing prismatic streams, and there are as many colors as there are forms it can take. Experiencing that beauty is beyond the scope of your duty. Understand, this ethereal energy is the same that charges emotions and constitutes ghosts, memories. It is the enigmatic muse that inspires artists.

"Know this: blood is the medium in which this ether moves and is stored. When it has an imbalance of humors, it is diseased. It cannot accept or transmit more power than it had originally. As sorcerers and artists exercise creativity, they will deplete this source. Dyscrasiac blood can be drained, and does not replenish. The iron elements within it turns color, as you see it, from red, to blue, to a black oil. Blood is a like a water well, students. When diseased, it will run dry. The amount of sorcery is then limited by the amount of blood available. And thousands have been sacrificed. As the extinct elders grew sick and battled for life, we required amounts of energy that only large scale sacrifices could provide. This is why your parents died. They were sacrificed for the ether in their blood."

He paused, seeing his audience collectively remember, seeing their memories reconstruct as crimson nightmares about them, visions of kidnapped fathers, impaled mothers in the blood bogs…

When they were ready to listen again, he continued. "The true victory of the Gray Lords was harmonizing the ratio of elements in their blood, ceasing the ill reactions to dyscrasia. This reversal was an outcome of Lysis saving the hybrid Echo from the Queen's Forge. It was then that the alchemical elements of earth and ether were brought into balance.

"Ever since, expressing creativity enriches the blood of the Grays. They depend on your artisanal offerings for strength, but not your blood or the blood of others. The amount of energy provided is limited only by the emotive limits of your work. When they feed, the fiery ether of their blood changes, from black, to colored, to brilliant white. Blood is a like a water well, as I have said. When healthy, it can be refilled with rain."

Then he used his cleaver's hilt as a gavel, banging it into the table to focus everyone's attention.

"This is your charge, as inkers and curators," Doctor Grave proclaimed, "to empower your Lords. The beauty you create feeds their energy source. Your primary duty, will be to protect their blood. If they are cut in battle, bind their wounds as a curator. If they become drained of energy, empower them with your art."

By the end of that lesson, his cut had sealed itself.

Helen's awareness shifted back to the present. It was clear now that Echo's hybrid blood needed charging. He needed an inker to help him.

A cluster of women jested that attending to the lesser demigod was a sentence worse than being imprisoned in Lysis' dungeon. They dreaded the prospect of serving the Gray Foundling:

"Lord Lysis is so much more regal, a human promoted to god...but Echo is so—"

"Passive... inhuman—"

"He looks like the imprisoned creatures—"

"He has only one curator and one guardian... Lysis has scores of each—"

"Foundling Echo just listens...and stares...he does not lead—"

"Lord Lysis allows him only one curer for a reason..."

Helen was enraged. Lord Echo was an equal Gray, Lysis did not reign over him! Years ago, right before Sharon joined Echo's side, she told Helen that the Lord Foundling dreaded being a burden to others—even us lesser humans. He needed at least one inker, and she went to him willingly. Unlike the esteemed Lysis, who demanded servitude from an army.

As it was, Helen need not worry about Lysis reading her mind since he was not present in the Theater. He, his regiment of inkers, and his undead warrior horde were patrolling the Land outside the Chromlechon Keep, pursuing demonic creatures. After the hunt, he would undoubtedly return with a carcass, or perhaps a living specimen for Doctor Grave to imprison and dissect. So numerous were his missions in which his ranks suffered, once a lunar cycle the initiate inkers would come here and observe Lord Lysis as he selected replacements. Today the routine varied, since this ceremony was for the 'lesser' Gray.

Gray Echo stood beside his dying servant, his guard,

and the Doctor. The demigod held Sharon's hand. As her soul departed, her last bit of artwork disappeared from the flag blanketing her corpse. Echo's tattoos faded further. Echo had drained all the ink of any substance from both fabric and flesh. Exhausted, his back drooped. He needed an infusion soon.

No one, including the Doctor, expected the standard fanfare of Lysis' succession ceremonies. Echo would not select or demand a replacement, but what would he do? Doctor Grave prodded via telepathy, *"Lord Gray, shall we proceed with a call to order? I will assist in—"*

"Wait, Doctor. Do you not see what happens when humans are forced to accompany me? How can I ask someone to sacrifice her life?"

"Forced? Bryhan here gave his life willingly to you. As did your healer."

"Yes," agreed the Guard. *"But Sharon and I volunteered. He did not request our service."*

The Doctor advised, *"Without a replacement, my Lord, you will weaken. Perhaps die. Your undead friend Bryhan would collapse. What else can you choose to do?"*

"I choose not to be a parasite."

Doctor Grave rearranged the fabric flag that covered most of Sharon's body. *"Lord Echo, you did not drain Sharon's soul. Some vampyric demon did. But once, you did feed as chaotically. Recall your youth? Before we learned to control the creation and consumption of color? Many were drained of life. You cannot deny your body's need to feed on the ethereal, but you have never been able to consume ether in a controlled manner."* The Doctor arranged Sharon's quills. *"You need a human medium. A healer."*

Echo waved his articulated arms in an arcane dance, he stirred Sharon's fluid soul. To the humans, his subject was invisible. In mere minutes, Echo conveyed to his deceased partner that she had passed on but her voice was needed.

"Lord, am I dreaming?" Sharon's soul awakened.

"No, Sharon, you have died. Protecting me…"

Her ghost floated beside her body. *"I am dead? Everything solid looks gray now, but there are colorful clouds flowing everywhere. It is a beautiful world, these memories and souls I now see."*

"It is a beauty that I wished you could never see."

She assessed the condition of her Lord. *"You survived the attack? But you have not completed the rite. You look weak. You need energy. Can I heal you as a ghost?"*

"Not now. I need another. Help me identify a curator. Someone like you."

Echo danced subtly in place. He granted Sharon's soul the energy needed to move further from her body and explore the chamber. He eased his actions to a calm sway, and surveyed the crowd. The humans in the Theater could not detect the sorcery. They remained active in their gossiping, oblivious.

Sharon's ghost responded. She sat upright. Hovering over the concentric pews, she inspected the neophytes as an invisible, inviscid entity. Helen's aura shined brightest. Sharon homed in on the ribbon she had given her, honored that it remained there.

Helen was compelled to caress the resonating thread. The myriad of ghosts attached to her other relics responded. The most coherent spirit was of her mother who interpreted and relayed the message cryptically: *"Helena, it is time to come home. Come now, down off the hill. Your friend visits our fireside."* A chorus of other spirits complemented the call and compelled Helen forward. Her muses thus became an extension of her senses, transmitting the emotion of Sharon's spirit. Helen's intuition rarely failed her. Decidedly, Helen rose.

She glided through the shadows, down the side staircase, toward the center stage, her hands at to her sides, feeling the nonexistent prairie grass of her dreams fold in her wake. Sharon attempted to hold Helen's left hand, to guide her.

The Gray Foundling, his Guard, and the Doctor stepped backward to acknowledge the body of ghosts about her.

Echo addressed Sharon, *"You seem attached to this candidate. She will be facing the same harm that killed you. I may not be able to protect her from death."*

"Lord, you taught me that death is not an end, now I see that. And death awaits all of us red bloods. Before our end, we are blessed with opportunities to experience life. I know that she seeks as you do. She cannot be fulfilled seeking within the Keep's confines. Serving you may free her."

Dazed, Helen asked, "What happened? Why, Masters, do you step away?" The act of speaking awakened her a bit. How did she get so close to the dais? Her face flushed. "Forgive me, I was mesmerized. I will return to my seat at once."

"Stay," Echo commanded. "We merely accommodate

what you cannot *see*. You hardly walk alone. A parade of muses accompany you." Echo then calmed Sharon's ghost. The emotive spell subsided. Sharon's ghost quietly came to terms with her condition. She groped about trying to touch her paints to no avail. Her soul was anchored to the body she could not touch. Confused, she remained sitting on the table, her invisible legs dangling, awaiting for death to make sense to her.

Helen approached her dead friend. Grave observed her critically, but her presence was readily accepted by Echo and Bryhan.

From this intimate vantage, Helen could see that Sharon's body was depleted of color. Her once brilliant, red hair was now gray throughout, and her eyes had blackened so that the iris was no longer distinct. Her tattoos lost all hint of indigo. No redness persisted in her flesh. So desiccated was her skin, Helen half expected it to crumble upon her touch like cold cinders.

Seeing Sharon's body, the gravity of her choice set in, for Helen did not understand the full extent of the Gray Foundling's powers. Had Echo drained Sharon's body? Did Sharon become consumable art?

Then her training countered her fear, and she began to trace an intricate pattern on Sharon's cheeks. Helen did not draw with styli or quills like the others. She had groomed her nails to perform those functions. Some folded lengthwise to draw liquid in their channels; others were flatter but curled axially, designed to scrape. Her inventory of tools was thus dynamic, various tips occasionally breaking while, over time, she formed others into intricate implements. Some she chewed constantly to keep pliant.

"Do you seek to succeed where I could not?" inquired Doctor Grave, his words seeping through his hood like smoke. "Raising the dead is a not a human art. Nor are you even a surgeon. With your limited powers, what do you expect to do?"

"Masters, I ink only to ease her soul, not to reanimate. I feel her soul needs to know that another human cared for her. That her path in life was worth following."

You should know about her then, Echo was prepared to say. *She liked to pick flowers when we ventured.* He read Helen's thoughts and decided not to speak. He silently watched memories resurface in her mind as she stared at Sharon. *You know her already.*

Next to Sharon were her ink bladders. Helen pricked a bladder with her index finger, and out seeped red ink. She laid down a flowing swirl. She wove trails of ink into lengthy ribbons. Stick figurines, dressed in skirts, strung together hand in hand, covered the surface of Sharon's face, as did flowering vines. Under Sharon's left ear, beneath a lock of hair, Helen scribed the word: Sharon. Then she leaned forward and whispered, "Farewell."

The art faded immediately, first losing hue, then form, as if the ink was comprised of smoke. She had never witnessed the consumption of ink so vividly before.

Helen continued to draw. The red slowly fading to gray. She knew Echo was not feeding on her art since his body did not rejuvenate. Something else inside Sharon had consumed

Helen's offering. Something competed for the color. Helen drew more, and from red to translucent gray they waned. Anticipating the color change now, Helen continued.

"Your art is indeed comforting her soul," undead Bryhan added. "But we are here to find a replacement, and you have stepped forward. You follow a dangerous road, perhaps to your death."

Sharon's death did not scare Helen away. Death was inescapable. It surrounded them all. Even here, things routinely died on this very stage. The bogs surrounding the Keep reeked of death. The promise of life was elsewhere. Beyond the Keep. But the Land was not safe yet. Lord Lysis still patrolled. It had been twenty years since she had been abroad. She mulled over her possible futures. Sharon had ventured forth. Following her seemed more natural than staying here. "Yes. I will take her place and wherever that leads me, if you will accept."

Echo inquired, "Why?" in an effort to evaluate her sincerity.

Helen dipped her fingernails to keep them from shaking. "I have more in common with Sharon than anyone else here. I feel drawn to her now. To her mission." She studied Echo. She saw loneliness in his eyes. By his intense gaze, she knew that he assessed her own aura. She wanted to be understood as much as he needed a healer. "And I am not scared of you, Foundling Gray. Would you accept me as her replacement?"

After Helen spoke, her rational mind caught up with the consequences of her proposal. She was hardly prepared for service. She was committing herself to creating impermanent art, tattoos that would be consumed by Echo as he healed or cast spells and maintained his Guard's life. She was to sustain the hybrid Foundling that fed not on meat, but on ethereal creations.

"And who asks to serve me?"

Helen was confused.

Guard Bryhan leaned close. She saw the white blood animating him glowing beneath his leathery, corpse skin. He explained, "You know our names, initiate, but we know not yours."

Quivering and breathless, Helen attempted to clear her throat. *My name is Helen.* But she was unable to say it aloud. If she could not speak her own name, then why should anyone else be expected to? It was as if her identity was gradually being absorbed into the vacuum of anonymity. *Who am I?*

"Helena…," Echo spoke suddenly, reading her mind, and awakening her abruptly. Her heart began racing as her name resonated in the chamber. She now realized that she had been on the brink of becoming nameless, a free roamer without purpose, and then she found herself on this stage. Echo had restored her. "Where is your flag, Helena?"

Embarrassed that she forgot her canvas, she blushed. She imagined it folded atop her sleeping quarters in the lower tunnels, abandoned in the dark. Her mind reeled, seeking an alternative canvas. Doctor Grave had taught that any medium could transmit creative works into magical power. Her flag was merely a formal conduit in which to offer it. Any canvas could suffice in practice. She pulled the pelt from her shoulders.

Bryhan held his hand up to decline. "That is more than

a mere flag," he said, reading the garment's aura. "That pelt is yours alone. You need not sacrifice something so special. But you should have a canvas on which to spell."

Helen looked around for a flag. Sharon was covered in one, but taking hers was unacceptable. She regained her composure. "I am without a flag. But you are weak and it is not necessary. May I tend to you without it?"

The Gray Foundling gestured approvingly. She began scrawling on Echo's right shoulder. She chose to delineate a portrait of Sharon on his chitin hide, using a mixture of mustard yellow and cinnabar to represent Sharon's original hair. A floral swirl wrapped the effigy, as if she swam in a field of flowers. Echo drank in the creative expression. Her offering soaked into the Gray's body and soul. The confines of the chamber melted away as she worked, until the Gray Foundling was sufficiently healed to stand as straight as his thorax permitted, and his Guardian was strengthened enough to carry Sharon's body. Sensing her work was complete, she fiddled with Sharon's ribbon for inspiration. Helen supposed Echo's lack of relics affected him. She raised an eyebrow. Where would he put one? He had no hair or clothes, after all. He acted human, but clearly was not.

Guard Bryhan communicated, *"Lord, she is looking at your absence of trinkets. Your body is bare. She wonders why you have none."*

"And what connection to the worldly do I have, Bran? I am not of the human culture."

"No ornament is necessary, Helena. You have healed me

with your arts," Echo whispered. "I need a curer. Will you join my cadre?"

"Yes, my Lord." Helen felt an energetic rush, her muscles and cheeks swelling with heat. She was giddy with euphoria. Pride. Purpose. This bond between curator and a Gray Lord entwined their spirits; such connections, emotional chains, were not permanent; but breaking them would be costly. She grew excited to serve even though she did not know the particulars of his mission yet. Intuition had led her onto a mysterious path.

To his new partner, Echo said, "You belong now, Curator Helena." To the masked golem, he pronounced, "Doctor Grave, I have found my inker."

Grave replied, "Shall I dismiss the neophytes, Lord?"

"Yes, Doctor."

Doctor Grave escorted the initiates away. In truth, the unselected Keepers were thankful that someone they did not intimately know had volunteered. Their expected fate to serve Lysis remained on course. As it was, they left breathing collective sighs of relief and dismissive curses as they hustled out:

"That ceremony was hardly proper—"

"I did not know the selection process even started…"

"Crazy misfit. She just walked right up there uninvited…"

"Who but an improper woman would volunteer to serve the lesser Gray?"

Meanwhile, Echo's band prepared to leave the Theater too. *"Sharon, your loyalty has overwhelmed me. It pains me, but we must find a place to rest your body, to let it complete its journey toward the earth from which it sprang."*

"Lord, over ten years you have taken me across the Land to many places during your search. You freed my mind from being mired in the past...shown me countless beautiful landscapes..."

"Where shall your body go amongst all those places?"

"I would like Helen to see City Tonn as soon as she can, so she can learn that humanity outside the Keep is recovering. Please take her there for me. Leave me there, for if not by your side, I belong there with the Outsiders. In Tonn's catacombs."

"We will go there immediately."

Echo nodded toward Sharon. "Bran?" Bryhan understood and moved to collect her body. He wrapped the flag about it, preparing it for travel. Then he lifted her gracefully over his shoulder.

To all, Echo said, "We must go. The situation is urgent. The demons responsible for Sharon's death remain. After we lay her body to rest, we will investigate the source of this new danger."

"Lord, does not Lysis hunt them now?" asked Helen.

Bryhan explained, "Yes, while Lord Lysis is hunting, we must seek."

"I'll need to get my paint," Helen said. "And my flag."

"Go then to your chambers with haste, Helena," Echo commanded. "Meet us atop the South Gate ramparts."

THE AIR WAS thinner and blustery atop the fortification, a dramatic change from the stagnant atmosphere of the Keep's core. Echo, Bryhan, and Helen followed the crenulated parapet while fighting blasts of wind. Periodic gusts would rapidly swell Helen's fabric banner, pushing her about between each merlon. The cold bit her exposed skin..

After a time, she disconnected the flag from its stave and furled it about herself. The staff became a hiking stick to brace herself against the gales.

Helen addressed the Sky, "I am not going back down into the tunnels. Just accept me as I am." The wind responded by shoving her and whipping her braids into her face as if to test her resolve. Despite her detachment from the others in the Chromlechon, she had become acclimated to its environment.

The outside proved strange and unwelcoming. The light from the sun abated only with passing clouds. The periodic flickering of brightness gave Helen a headache. She had spent most of her life living in the darkness of the Keep's core. Now the sun looked upon her with hostility.

She traveled with her scant possessions attached. A dozen bladders of pigments hanging from twine bounced around her hips. Ballooned within were oily pastes of ground lapis, tempered cinnabar, and other mulled minerals. Her pelt mantled her neck beneath the flag.

The trio made their way to South Gate in a line, Echo in front and Bryhan carrying Sharon's corpse before Helen. He moved to stand between her and the wind. She appreciated this gesture and fell into step within his shadow. His stride did not seem affected by the air current, even as he lumbered with Sharon. Unlike Doctor Grave whose flesh appeared ceramic, Bryhan's flesh was like dried leather stretched over his skeleton. His left arm did not match the texture or color of the rest of his body. It was an artificial limb; the original had been detached when Bryhan fought a demon defending his mother. He had lost that battle. Bryhan remained one-armed throughout the end of the Ill Age, even as he dived into the bogs to rescue the mysterious, young Foundling. Bryhan died while saving Echo, and was eventually reanimated by him.

Echo walked at a brisk pace. Helen strived to keep up with Byrhan, who followed. She had little idea of their mission apart from the need to bury Sharon soon. "Guard Bryhan?"

"Curator Helena, please call me Bran." A breeze muffled his voice. Bryhan's lamellar armor glistened in the morning sun. It was meticulously crafted from a rare, white serpent's hide, wyvern scales.

"I will call you Bran, if you call me Helen."

"Very well."

Helen began again, "Bran, what comes next?"

He balanced himself with the iron spear in his left hand, the body on his right shoulder. Clutching the stanchion, the guard extended his index finger over the brick and voiced something. The wind howled in her ears so loudly that she could not hear his words.

Helen looked over the wall to see the panoramic vista. Given the Keep's position atop a mountain, the scene was breathtaking. Far away to the east, the horizon was lined with two mountain ranges. The colorful, sandstone stripes of the Arenites stretched from the South; it looked like a library, each slanted strata of crystalline mineral being another book bound of varied hue: bone-white, ocher red, sulfur yellow, and lapis blue. Many Keepers imagined it as a crystallized rainbow: solidified Sky. North and West of the sandy Arenites was the white-peaked Calx range, a zenith of limestone; its grey surface blended seamlessly with smooth, sparse glaciers.

Bryhan hailed from the Clan Tonn, which was nestled between these mountains. Was he pointing toward his homeland now? What of her origin? The highlands she once called home were to the northeast. Instinctively, she tried to orient herself by locating the now desolate district of Clan Qual. The rolling hills she remembered appeared flat from here.

Her line of travel along the ramparts compelled her to look into the neighboring wasteland: the bogs, where the bodies of the Keepers' ancestors rotted long ago. Revolted, Helen tried to look away from the shallow sea of melancholy. The wetland was bereft of life. It wrapped the Chromlechon Keep like a moat, being more expansive in the south. Thousands had died there, and their remains had all decayed or had been turned to stone by untamed geomancy.

"Must the Land be so desolate?" Helen asked the wind. She longed to admire some man-made edifice. Even ruins would reveal some vestige of humanity. The black oil of the bogs was a desolate substance, presenting no human relic for an empathetic person to connect with. It was the absence of art.

She had been taught that the oil was dense with emotions and soul: liquefied oblivion. The decay contained a lot of emotive power, yet it would release none of it. It could only absorb it.

Suddenly, a trail of glittering sparks caught her eye.

Far below, what looked to be a colossal iridescent snake was slithering its way through the countryside toward the exterior of the Chromlechon. It undulated and heaved as if swallowing some prey whole. The tail section was gray and barbed, several lengths longer than the rainbow colored hood. The front of the beast curved up the ramps of scree toward the fortification. Helen observed the serpent's rear separating from the head, diffusing completely into the Gray Orchard, a forest comprising thousands of impaled demons, skeletons, and creatures. The illusion thus revealed itself. This was not a snake but the Gray Horde, Lysis' warriors, riding atop soldier ants, the light reflecting off their armor. What appeared to be the serpent's layered frill fanned and contracted rhythmically. Scores of brilliantly-decorated standard-bearers continued toward South Gate.

Now Lysis returned from Cypria's caldera in the northwest, where Sharon had been attacked. Cypria's Gallwomb was a sacred place, at least for Echo. It was where Gray Foundling was born, when Lord Lysis opened the demigod's womb. A litter of hybrid creatures had been freed, Echo among them. Clouds of volcanic ash rolled across the countryside. Wildfires erupted. The earth shook. Echo contemplated the source of the hybrids, *Were pathways to the Otherworld opened with my birth?*

Gray Lysis returned from his hunt by the same path

Helen used to leave. He had been successful. Three captive prey were retrieved from the wild. The still, monstrous heaps encumbered the insectan mounts. Dead? Unconscious?

Echo looked over the ramparts, but he gazed more distantly. With the powers of *sight* afforded to him by his mysterious birth, he spied the landscape. Leagues beyond the limit humans could see, Echo spotted dispersing ribbons of astral fire, which meandered through the far away forests. Miles and miles separated these signatures. Somewhat central was the district of Clan Tonn, but the threat was too sparse to draw conclusions. *For every creature you catch, Lysis, another emerges.*

Echo, Bryhan, and Helen descended into the courtyard. A rush of heat hit them. Smoke blew up Helen's nose and gagged her. Embers sparkled in the wake of the plume, assuming the aspect of little creatures. They flickered, changing shape continuously. Furies and sprites fluttered about like brilliant butterflies. Some entirely made from flame. Others merely singed paper. One landed on Helen momentarily, only to spring off and realign with the current of the dispersing smoke column.

Lysis' prismatic Pyre lay ahead. Lesser artists streamed in and out of porous walls, orderly formations going to immolate folios in this bonfire: portraits of Lysis, depictions of their nightmares, hopes and dreams. The minerals used in the paints burned remarkably; they created fascinating, multicolored flames for both living and the undead to see. Remains of the smoldering papers flurried about the courtyard. Ghostly elements, such as emotive energy, were not conserved quantities like energy or mass; the beauty involved with creating and appreciating art could instantly materialize, dissipate, explode or collapse without measure. This creative source birthed the fire sprites. Impermanent, luminous creations. Autonomous. Crawling out from under ashes. Animated minions of limited magic and life. Hundreds of glowing sparks rode the smoke clouds. Minions of Lord Lysis. Parchment fragments folded into winged shapes: miniature phoenixes, fairies, and wyrms. Bearers of his invitations.

It was fortunate that Lysis relied on surrogate criers to lure orphans here, Helen considered. Lord Lysis did protect those who answered the call. But had he been the messenger, she would not have come. Nor would any scared urchin. Who would answer a call to a walking skeleton? Lysis appeared to be as monstrous as the prey he hunted.

A fairy cat that dripped cuprous flames darted toward Helen, encircling and rubbing against her legs. She brushed it away to avoid catching on fire. The feline sprite returned to nibble on her flag. Admittedly it was not the same exact sprite that had brought her and Sharon here, but it played directly on her needs to escape the horrors of life. To find a family in which to belong. Was this sprite confused? "Oh I see. You know that Sharon and I are leaving. Do you not remember having brought us here already? We came. Grew. But it is time to depart." She shooed it away. "Go find another to save."

The cat turned its head, listening. It arched its back, and sprung over the ramparts, carried by the Sky.

South Gate's architecture wrapped around the immense promontory. Seen from outside the Keep, it appeared like a large nose protruding from the pinnacle of the Chromlechon Mountain. From inside the walls, the threshold was a grand aperture centered in the ground. Ascending or descending the opening required a special mount capable of crawling steep, vertical slopes. The courtyard had no roof, but at this elevation, even gargoyles had difficulty flying; there were no known enemies that could clear it.

Around the Gate's base were many holes sinking into the Keep. From these, colossal ants crawled out with purpose, arranging themselves at regular intervals around the horizontal portcullis. They grabbed links of chain with their mandibles and retracted to open the Gate.

Up from the cavity, emerged Gray Lord Lysis leading his caravan. The mere sight of Lysis made Helen anxious. His antlered head and skull-face were as threatening as the tusked insect he rode: the once-Queen of the Chromlechon. He had usurped his mount. Now he rode upon her as if she were a warhorse. Her colony had originally carved the tunnels of the Keep. She had ruled over thousands of eldritch ants, hundreds of golems like Doctor Grave. So great was Lord Lysis' power, he quelled the former Queen's dyscrasiac sorcery and possessed her body.

Helen was nearer to Lysis than she had ever been in her life. Even with him atop the great insectan Queen, she could discern the various flayed faces covering his frame: a dozen expressions stitched together, their taut mouths twisted with the slightest movement, as if the ghosts of the original owners struggled to speak. As intimidating as his attire was, his death's head was most prominent. Her heart raced. She fidgeted with anxiety, inventorying her paint bladders with twitchy fingers.

Lysis turned to mindspeak with his fellow Gray. *"Cypria's opened gall is haunted. The ether there is toxic. These mutant creatures roamed there."*

"I believe they came from elsewhere," Echo proposed.

"You will want to scout your birthplace again in any event. Monitor the crags."

Echo nodded in agreement.

Lysis observed the bundle on Bryhan. *"Sharon did not survive the attack."*

Echo concurred. *"We go now to bury her in the Tonn Catacombs."*

"Beware, Echo, these vermin moved in organized patterns. They search for something." Lysis looked over the walls. *"There must be more of these white bloods out there."*

"I have surveyed the Land from this vantage. The threat appears minimal for now. Only a handful of creatures spread over many leagues. I deem you collected half of their numbers today from Cypria's Gall. I do not anticipate many more encounters."

Lord Lysis pointed toward his catch and spoke for all to hear, "Beware, these creatures bleed white." He moved aside, directing Echo to step forward, *"Confirm if one of them is Sharon's killer."*

Echo approached the specimens searching for Sharon's signature marking. He saw a face coalesce in the ether steaming from them. Translucent and white. Feminine. Her head was not round enough to be human. It was heart shaped with three inset jewels between her eyes. Her moist lips parted, but her voice was too hushed to hear. Echo turned toward his fellow Grays, yet Lysis and Bryhan did not take notice. He looked back toward the face, but it had dissipated. He strained his eyes, scrutinizing for traces of it. He had lost the ghost, but did see Sharon's mark.

"This one," Echo spoke aloud.

Curious, Helen neared the three hybrids. Curled up and netted within larvalwyrmen bundles, it was difficult to discern their true form. Half-human women, half-immense grasshoppers. The captives' fleshy upper bodies morphed into armored thoraxes. Their hindquarters were the size of horse's rumps, shielded in smooth plates. Each limb was patterned with tiger-like stripes, black and green. One prisoner had lost its rear left leg, and the empty joint was a glistening stump.

Echo did not notice Helen approach, being so engrossed inspecting the body.

"What are they? Why would he bring them here?" Helen whispered to Echo.

"Lysis often catches stray hybrids. Most are mutants, blue-blooded humans with wings or antennae. But these are chromanti, special hybrids that share similar white blood. None of us is certain of their origin. They could be the spawn of dyscrasia-ridden elders. However, Doctor Grave does not believe this to be true. Reproducing is too challenging for them. This catch poses a novel threat. In a sense, they are less dangerous, since their blood should not react with that of humans' or the Gray Lords'. On the other hand, we do not know much about their motivations."

Bran interjected, "See now, Doctor Grave comes to haul the surviving prisoners away for interrogation."

The golem was striding across the courtyard. "They are no threat now. They are unconscious." Grave adjusted the bonds, preparing to carry the bodies down to the prison. He paused to collect their blood into vials.

Echo came forward again to inspect the specimen. His antennae stroked the maimed chromantaur.

Suddenly, electric sparks arced.

A sac burst from within the hybrid.

Echo was driven into Helen, wet with acrid residue. The collision popped her indigo paint bladder, and it colored her right leg. Helen regained her footing to see Doctor Grave, Lysis, and Bryhan subduing the awakened, berserk chromantaur. It seized violently but without presence of mind. Bryhan anchored the tip of his iron spear into the neck of the female creature, holding her at a safe distance as Lysis' magical sword *Ferrus Eviscamir* sliced three times for every instance Grave swung his grand cleaver.

The she-beast reared awkwardly on its surviving hind leg. Beneath its breasts a symmetric pattern was displayed: a circle with six rays. It was not a natural pattern like the stripes on its legs. The symbol was a signature blazon, a brand. Helen cringed as its naked chest was cut open, its shallow cleavage split vertically, and the sun-like brand divided. A subsequent strike cut the body further, opening its exposed thorax and spilling entrails.

Shrieks rang out from the demon. White blood crackling with lightning gushed out.

"Lord Echo!" Helen gasped. *Lapis elixir* cascaded off her fallen master.

The white gore reeked like fish. Helen knew that the liquid would affect him in some way. She gagged as she reached for him. She washed it from Echo's skin with her flag. It was chalky and gritty, similar to wet sand—just as the Doctor had described in his lessons. These new hybrids did share the same eucrasiac blood! To her surprise, all the pearly ichor wiped relatively easily off Echo. The fluid left an oily mark upon his flesh. The blast of liquid had knocked him over, but he was otherwise unharmed.

With her nails, she scraped up the paint that had splattered upon her legs. She scrawled images over the dark marks left by the ichor on Echo's body. She worked without cleansing herself of the spray, which left similar stains onto her already mottled hands. The color bleached from her design as both Echo and the chromantaur's blood competed for the creative power.

The Gray Foundling stared intently into the air, almost hypnotized by some ghost. Strange astral smoke emanated from wherever the ichor had contacted his flesh. However, the substance was so fleeting Echo was not sure they were real.

Doctor Grave came over to inspect him. *"Your aura connected with that of the creature. What did you do?"*

"I worked no sorcery intentionally."

Grave spoke aloud, "The chromantaur's injury must have built up internal pressure, some slow reaction that required a mere touch to trigger its release."

"To the dungeon with them, Grave," Lysis commanded. "We'll interrogate them when they are contained behind iron." The liverymen arrived, commanding their larvalwyrmen to transport the chromanti below ground.

Advancing toward her, Lysis scrutinized Helen from his vantage atop the once-Queen. Helen's eyes met his black void sockets. The empty cavities captivated her. Frozen in place, she stared as his invisible magic connected with her mind. Threescore of his healers and warriors inspected her from behind him. A telepathic discussion occurred among those who worked Gray powers. Helen could not hear, but she could almost feel their ethereal whispering in her bones.

She was being judged. By Lysis. His entourage.

The telepathic conversation ended.

The once-Queen advanced toward Helen with deliberation, her grace demonstrated the standard poses of heraldry precisely: first striding to a halt before Helen, then rotating her head to align their eyes, gazing statically for a pause, then lowering her rear four legs courteously to sit with an erect thorax, and finally lowering her forelegs to lie.

Lysis dismounted and strode toward Helen. She struggled to rise. Bryhan helped her to stand.

Sheathed on Lysis' back was his mystical sword, *Ferrus Eviscamir*. The sword was reputed to cut through any material, be it stone, bone, or metal. In his hands, it could carve gorges into the Land, or vacuums of space in the Sky. Nevertheless, Lysis needed no weapon to terrify his adversaries. His own appearance was enough. One glance at his figure was sufficient evidence of every myth concerning his transformation from man, to possessed skeletal warrior, to Gray Lord. His body had suffered the price of wrestling with sorcery and gods. Wrought tendrils of bone crowned his head like antlers. Gnarled strands of bleached hair hung from the sides of his bare skull. He had earned his role as supreme leader of the all the dispossessed children of the Land. The community relied upon his command for two decades. Even after he had seized control over the forces of dyscrasia, the source of the disease remained at large, and threats of hybrid creatures persisted.

The demon killer stood before Helen. He looked at her intently. "Your new healer. She lacks something," Lord Lysis pronounced with resonating depth.

Lacked something? How about everything? Helen thought. Uncertain, standing there with paint and gore dripping down her legs.

"Bring her a beacon." Lysis directed his subordinates. One of his artists rushed to prepare a brand in the Pyre. She decorated the torch with heavy stripes of mineral paint: cupric verdigris green, ferrous blue vitriol, mercuric red vermillion, and arsenic yellow. Suffused with energy from the Pyre, it burned wondrously. Then the skeletal Lord grasped it. Flames wrapped his tempered bones. White blood oozed from within his grip, hallowing the torch. He extinguished it. In a moment, it was cool enough for Helen to accept, primed with his magic.

"Your fear is warranted. Danger is abroad." Lord Lysis leaned toward Helen, "Light the brand, call my name, and I will come."

Helen was awestruck. She had expected his behavior to match his dark appearance. Yet he offered her a means for assistance. She had trouble reconciling his intimidating presence with his desire to protect. So much so, she could not speak until he exited the courtyard.

As Lysis descended into a hole, Helen confessed to Echo, "Lord Lysis scared me more than the prisoners."

"He has honored you by speaking aloud, at least in part. He did not need to communicate audibly since all here can converse through the ether."

A man robed with an enormous collar materialized from the livery leading the reins of an insectan mount. The insect's exoskeleton was filled with undead wyrms animated by sorcery. Unlike those of Lysis' company, this soldier mount was bareback and unarmored.

Bryhan noticed Helen's confused expression. "We must travel cautiously and speedily, so we must ride."

"Bran, what do I ride?"

"Helena, if you follow Sharon's way, you will prefer my back over that of the soldier ants." Echo explained, kneeling.

Ride the Gray Foundling? She had never mounted an eldritch creature, let alone a Gray. Echo remained low. The collared man boosted her into position atop Echo's thorax.

They cantered toward the Gate. Bryhan and his tusked solider walking side by side with his companions.

Adjusting her flag shawl to shield her from the wind, Helen asked, "Master Echo, where do we go?"

Echo sensed something and did not respond. Helen turned toward Bryhan questioningly.

Bryhan explained. "Take no offense. The Lord can appear aloof when he engages with the spirit realm. Even with my undead sight, I cannot detect what he does. But look there. See his antennae vibrate? That happens when he is focused."

Helen observed the wispy appendages. She was just beginning to learn what was normal behavior for the Foundling. Now she knew to watch his antennae more closely.

"To answer your question, we go to the Tonn Mines. To bury Sharon."

This perplexed Helen further. "But her family had been from Clan Qual. Why are we not taking her there?"

"Qual was devastated, and no one has tried to rejuvenate it. After she joined us, she began to grow attached to Tonn. She became friends with the Outsiders there. They are suspicious of the Keep and struggle to rebuild. Weather and demons haunt them on occasion. She befriended and healed many during our wayfaring. She desires to be buried there."

Helen had never been to City Tonn. Surely it had to be a grand complex with everlasting architecture. It had been created by artisans who mastered stone and glass, after all. She imagined many edifices able to survive the volcanic Ill Age including basalt monoliths and colossal sculptures of kings. "There really are people out there in the wild? And Sharon healed them?"

"Yes," Echo said. "Some are unwilling to leave their homeland for the Keep. We confer with these Outsiders for information. Sharon's primary role was to sustain me, but she felt compelled to help any injured."

"I suppose I may do the same."

Bryhan said, "You are permitted, of course. Mind you, Echo's welfare is our key focus. Your creativity gives greater substance to his aura. When you contribute to Echo's skein of energy, it will restore me too. Without his powers, my body would collapse and decay. My soul could no longer communicate with the living. Even if he does not possess your body as he does mine, you will become attached to his spirit. If Echo's aura is damaged, you may be hurt too."

Helen wrapped the flag tighter about herself.

Then they descended, leaving the Keep's protection.

The grinding portcullis sealed them out, as the force of gravity pulled her down into the valley. Helen saw their destination in the far distance, beyond the bogs and forest, across the expansive gorge. There, the metal artisans and lapidaries once resided, beside mountains where they quarried for stone and ore; the exhausted mines doubled as catacombs. Death awaited them...

HELEN CLUNG TIGHTLY to Echo's neck while straddling his thorax. Bryhan rode beside them on a tusked eldritch soldier ant. They crossed a causeway of sodden land straddling the bog's shores, connecting the scree under South Gate to the surrounding vale. This led them toward the ancient trade way along the adjacent valley's trough: the Gorgepath.

Helen refused to look at the bogs. Had she been less superstitious, she could have discerned the paper mill beneath the Chromlechon Falls, which was out of sight from South Gate. The Grotto Folk lived above it and manufactured the materials for the curators' rites. The exterior of the Keep was speckled with their caves. She did hear the mill though. She relied on its creaking as a measure of distance between her and the bogs she disdained. She feared that the blackwater could suck out her soul through open eyelids. With them shut, her mind was sealed off—or so she hoped. Now that the putrescent smell of tar subsided, and the mill was no longer audible, her nose began to itch with the scents of grass and pine. The safety of the forest embraced them. She relaxed her grip a bit. Raising her eyes, she saw her master's neck, and focused on the future.

What awaited her? Where would Echo take her? Fantasy adventures took form. At first, imaginary landscapes grew. Long-stemmed grasses sprouted overhead, extending toward the Sky, their tips beyond reach. Wind swayed all. Sunlight retreated from shadows, flickering as a storm brewed. She cowered on Echo's back. Then creatures came. From the ground, glowing miniature arachnids emerged. Lava dripped from the crawlers. They shed burning, steaming soil as they escaped the earth's core. Climbing the grasses, the dense prairie ignited. Smokey wraiths flew from the burning grass, and chased after them. The insects grew in the flames, transforming into white-hot chromanti that gave chase…

Riding beside her, Bryhan watched Helen's daydream.

Echo, Helen's imagination is getting the better of her emotions. She thinks we are being hunted now. Bran looked over at his quiet master. Echo was immersed in thought, ruminating on his birth. His entry into the world coincided with his mother's death. He was last in the line of dyscrasiac mutants. He had no family, let alone any friends of like-body. On the one hand, he did not empathize or sympathize with the creatures Lysis hunted. And still he was not human, like the Keepers. He had no proper place, which motivated the search for one.

Bryhan realized that he would have to focus his master too. The Guard intervened telepathically, *Lord, perhaps we should tell her more about our purpose.*

Echo finally noticed that Helen was clinging rather tightly to him. *Of course, Bran.* He continued to travel as he spoke, "Helena, your creativity is strong."

"I was thinking about the creatures you track for Lysis." Helen relaxed her grip as the conversation disintegrated her visions of fiery cataclysm.

"True, I often track prey, since my sight is unsurpassed. We cooperate, but he needs no help from me to protect the Land. He carves his own path, guided by an internal drive and limitless power." *My goals are independent and less clear. My own body seems to have a destiny that reveals itself year after year incrementally as I molt. I do not know my final form, direction, or destiny. Despite your willingness to serve me, I lead you into the unknown. You follow me, Helena. But I know not where we go.*

Helen continued thinking about the chromanti. Her

Lord resembled the shape of the beasts Lysis had captured, but he was civilized and kind. "Lord, if Lysis does not direct you, how do you know where to go?"

"We are free to explore the entire Land. After we bury Sharon, we will return to where I originated, the opened Gallwomb of Cypria."

"The Gall?" She gulped. The Gall's bursting was the volcanic event that had erased her family. The calamity brought the end of the Ill Age, and gave way to the taming of dyscrasia that plagued the Land. "I have only heard stories about it."

Bryhan added, "You will see it soon with your own eyes."

"Yes, very soon, Bran. My ritual molting was inter-rupted. We need to go back."

Bryhan nodded. *"And should we inform her now?"*

"Yes, Bran. Gradually, however, to avoid overwhelming her."

Unaware of the telepathy, Helen continued, "I cannot imagine earth erupting so violently. How do you explore such devastation?"

The Opened Gall appeared in his mind: a wide, shallow caldera with an irregular lake in the center. From up in the Sky, it was a decapitated shoulder, a vacated neck crowned with a rock tiara. A labyrinthine canyon persisted within. Some chasms were engorged with rainwater. Some, as narrow and deep, were dry. "The Land was torn asunder. But it has changed since, healing in parts with fresh vegetation. Chasms have eroded into greater crags that run so deep, sunlight cannot penetrate them."

Hidden in one of these corridors was Echo's molting chamber. Eggshells from his siblings had settled there. They radiated memories of his early youth inside the Gallwomb. They comforted him, as Helen's pelt did her.

"The ghosts of past remain there." *There is also a museum of sorts, tracking my condition. Shells of my ever-changing self.* He envisioned them, side by side, a succession of hollow bodies placed in series. One year's growth between each imago of Echo, each taller than its predecessor and less human—more like the infected hybrids. *Once my white ichor separated me from them. But ...now...*

Helen breathed deep, "We must return then, Lord. If that place comforts you."

Echo did not respond. *It once did. We must return regardless.*

"Those grounds have a haunted past. It is even more dangerous now," Guard Bryhan explained. "The spirit of the place is scarred with Sharon's injury, since she was attacked there. . ."

Helen looked upon Sharon's body, swaddled in cloth on Bryhan's mount. The body was moving rhythmically with the eldritch ant's gait. Otherwise, it was as still as a corpse should be.

"Lord, she is curious about what happened to Sharon."

"Tell her more, then. Be careful, since your account may scare her unnecessarily."

Bryhan began: "Curator Helen, we spend most of our time outside the Keep. Often we encounter blue-blooded demons, so finding a gargoyle in the Gall's crags was not a complete surprise. The circumstances could have been better, of course. We were vulnerable preparing for a ritual..."

"Go on, slowly."

"Lord Echo was meditating as he readied for his annual molting. He had already entered into a trance. Sharon was prepared to aid him, and I was on guard."

Meanwhile, Echo thought to himself: *I stood beside shells of my former self. My exuviated skeletons stared with empty eyes toward me, looking to ascertain if I awoke with some newfound purpose. And I always look back at them, hoping they had withheld a secret. But they never offered direction. I fear my future is determined by my past. The Ill Age remains alive within me.*

Helen clung more intensely to her master.

"A feasting gargoyle drug fresh prey into our chamber. At first, it was unaware we occupied the cavern. Echo remained deeply entranced. Sharon sat motionless. I readied myself to attack. The creature's back shielded our view from the heap it consumed, but the victim appeared to be a female human. I read the ether to determine if the victim was still alive. She was, barely. Her legs were hidden from view, and her soul plain, so I did not perceive that she was a mutant too."

Helen's heart raced. Her hands moved upward to cover her ears. She managed to will them to stay lowered, and listened intently as duty demanded. "The gargoyle saw us, and I advanced quickly. It scampered out. I pursued. It proved faster than I, so I let it go. When I returned I saw..."

Bryhan paused to consider how to relay the events. Meanwhile, Echo recalled it: *"In your absence, Bran, Sharon had inspected the female. She healed it. The white-blooded hybrid stood on insectan legs. Sharon called out for help. I was unable to move. Sharon was struck down as it approached me. She regained her footing and charged with her standard as if it were a lance, and missed. A second strike knocked her senseless. Her aura dimmed then, as her blood sprayed onto the rocks about, forever staining the earth."*

"What did you see?" Helen asked Byrhan.

He turned to Echo for concurrence to proceed. "In my absence, Sharon must have revived the gargoyle's prey. It was not human after all, but what we are now calling a chromantaur. Rejuvenated, the hybrid had incapacitated her. It turned toward Echo when I returned."

I could do nothing. Frantic, I strove to emerge from my statuesque state. I watched that creature strike her down. She had healed it, and it betrayed her kindness.

"We fought immediately. It fled, injured. I would not risk leaving my Lord and the injured Sharon vulnerable, so I did not give chase. We ceased the molting ritual prematurely and returned to the Keep. We did not anticipate finding a white-blooded hybrid outside our Keep. We did not know they even existed. Only the Gray Lords, and those they reanimated, have *lapis elixir* in them."

"When we were in the Theater, the markings I put on Sharon's body lost their color. Does that mean her aura was injured somehow, in addition to her body?"

"Yes, Helen. Her soul was corrupted when she had healed it, her spirit blending with a tainted one. Her poisoned body kept losing color and ether. We rushed to the Keep since we could not reverse the ailment. She finally died in the Theater."

Echo finally reentered the conversation, "As we left South Gate with you, Helena, Lysis returned with the beasts. I saw Sharon's mark on one. Her healing signature was abundantly clear." He paused, recalling how the beast had connected with him. How its soul resonated with his, and the body revived. Was he now infected? Echo then heard a mysterious, telepathic voice. He concentrated on it but it remained unintelligible.

Helen saw Echo's antennae twitch.

To Bryhan, Echo mind-spoke, *"What did you say?"*

"Lord? I said nothing."

Echo discounted the foreign voice. He often discerned phantasms others could not. He could not demystify all of them. Sharon should remain the focus, he affirmed. Like Helen, she had been born in Clan Qual which had been decimated in the Ill Age. Her closest human friends had been outside the Keep, in the abandoned district of Tonn. "We take Sharon to the City, so that she may rest in peace." *Then we shall return to the Gall to complete my transition. May fate turn me into something better than the monsters I resemble. Will I emerge from metamorphosis as something alien, or as someone else? What will I become?*

II: Death Rains on the Joyless City

L ORD LYSIS TURNED from his watch over the Land, toward South Gate's courtyard, where the Doctor approached. Somewhere far to the east, Echo's party roamed. The rising sun did little to reveal the landscape over which they ventured. Backlit, the Arenites and Calx ranges appeared as flat, black peaks. The forest in the gorge was veiled in shadow. The bogs below disappeared into the nothingness.

"Did your interrogations of the prisoners yield information?"

Grave's ax *Hewnmaw* and apron were coated with chromantaur gore. "Yes. One remains alive in the dungeon. It is too weak to escape the gibbet. Lord, you need to know that these white-bloods belong to the same ancestry."

"They are possessed then."

"No, my Lord. Their blood is their own. But these

drones are related."

"A colony?"

"Yes. The scarceness of chromanti belies their strength. Our enemy is larger and more organized than we once believed. They belong to a community, one that must be hidden. Strangely, they share the blood we thought was unique. They are more like us than any we have encountered before. Their queen, assuming they have one, may know of their fates. Wherever she may be, she is aware of us."

"But we know the Land well. There is no place for a large colony to have been hiding."

"Lord, their origin is a mystery remaining to be solved."

Lysis repositioned himself to stare over the ramparts, but he saw nothing.

Grave added, "There is more. These drones were encoded to locate and retrieve a great treasure. They have found and marked their target. However, they remain dissatisfied. Their treasure evades their possession. They do not fear us. Nor death. They fear losing their prize."

"Tell me what they search for."

"That I do not know. I consulted my once-Queen. She had warned us about these chromanti for years. It is difficult to communicate to her spirit. Nevertheless, I had no other resource to make sense of the chromanti biology. Her ghost remembers some fragments of elder past, but such memories may be corrupted by time."

"And?"

"When asked about the hybrids, she spoke cryptically

of purification and reproduction. The fact they have all been female lends credence to the notion that the latter—"

"Our enemy seeks a mate."

"Lord, that is my conjecture."

Lysis dismissed the Doctor. From the far east, fluttering over the canopy of green, approached one of his fiery sprites. Over the Gorgepath, through the barren bogs, up the steep slopes of the Chromlechon. Returning alone. Not leading any newcomer.

"You have a message for me."

The fairy landed on its Lord's outstretched forearm. Only a hand's breadth tall, the parchment creature fluttered its wings, the edges searing with fresh oxygen only to decay immediately. Soon its crisp body would disintegrate. Only its proximity to Lysis reignited its strength. Opening its twig-like arms, the minion showed its stained hands: white ichor.

"This is not Echo's blood. Nor is it mine." Lord Lysis saw hundreds of crawling enemies in the message. They must be infesting the abandoned mines, out of sight. He had searched some of the district before, but there were miles upon miles of caverns. He had missed them! Then it occurred to him. *"Echo goes into their den!"*

Descending into the courtyard, he unsheathed *Ferrus Eviscamir.* With an outstretched hand he signaled to his retinue that they would not be attending this sortie. His curators gave way, their pennants snapping in the wind as they retreated. He had no time to drag them along, for even as the fairy flew, his trip would consume many hours, and he knew not exactly where his enemies or comrades were. Only that he had to head toward the east. Toward Tonn.

Lord Lysis marched into his Pyre.

"Grave! Take heed, I am off." The Doctor was already within the Keep's interior, but acknowledged the announcement via the ether.

Embers flared as Lysis' presence stoked the flames. Having worked the Underworld Forge, this fire did no harm to him. His strength swelled as his body absorbed its energies. His death's-head brightened, illumined like a celestial star held captive in bone. His entire body glowed brilliant white. Twirling his sword about the fire, reciting the ancient, thaumaturgical language of golems, Lysis thus performed his rite. *Ferrus Eviscamir* spelled his commands into the ether with the fluidity of a dancer.

He called to Nature. The Land responded by releasing its life. Untold swarms of insects answered his summons from abroad. From the ashes beneath his feet came glowing beetles. From the bogs about the Chromlechon came dragonflies. From forest brush and chasms deep, came roaches, wasps, and iridescent flies.

They swarmed, and took him away.

He ascended into the morning Sky with an insect horde.

THE PARTY TRAVELED over the surface of the Land for three days and nights without incident, save Helen's constant battle with the elements. The sores on her feet healed even as bruises set in her thighs. She woke from a nap slumped against Echo's neck. Adjusting her eyes, the undead guard, riding nearby, came into focus.

"Bran looks troubled," She reported to Echo. Presently Bryhan's forehead pressed against his iron shaft, much to Helen's confusion since she could not see Lady Aleece's phantom as her companions could, nor could she read Bryhan's mind. Still she was intuitively aware of Bryhan's discomfiture. "His weapon affects him."

Echo inspected his guard's aura. The angelic golden ghost of Aleece rode on his spear, her translucent torso still transfixed by it. Her spirit fire flared as they neared their home, reinvigorated by her memories and Bryhan's memories of her. As her specter burned brilliantly, Bryhan's happiness conversely depressed to a dim blue. Aleece had been abducted here, plucked from his arms by a demon who rode the Sky. Bryhan had managed to find her corpse in Haemarr's Blood Bogs, impaled on this very spear.

"Helena, his mood darkens as we near our destination." Echo said, "The reanimated are overburdened by haunting memories of their past. Lysis and I, and those we possess, *see* it all. Emotion flows between living blood and soul," Echo recounted the Rule of Blood. "But they extend to artifacts too, such is the Rule of Relics: souls of the artist remain with their art. We see apparitions attached to items, memories anchored to locations, and emotions emanating from sentient creatures. The ghosts for Bryhan become stronger here, since he once lived in the Clan Tonn's City. Memories cling to people and diminish over time and distance, only to inflame souls again when reunited."

"The Doctor taught us the Rules of Stone, and the Rule of Blood and Ether. Will I need to learn and apply this Rule of Relics?"

It seems you do already. If only you could see yourself as we do. Your head is beautifully eclectic, each charm a sparkling ornament. Your feline pelt is alive, its head peers over your shoulder now.

"No, Helena." Echo continued: "Bryhan's father, Clanlord Kaiyn, and his mother, Lady Aleece, died by the Doctor's sorcery, as did most of the clan. Lady Aleece was sacrificed on that very spear to the once-Queen and her last spawn. Understand, Doctor Grave served her and her offspring, before Lysis overpowered the colony."

"The Doctor was an enemy?"

Echo confirmed with a nod. "He strived to stimulate dyscrasia rather than tame it."

This revelation shocked Helen. There was much she did not know about the arcane golem and the once-Queen. She reminisced about how the Doctor educated the women of the Keep. His lectures about arcane Rules raced through her mind. Then she fantasized. The manikins in the Theater transformed into fleshy corpses. Her human counterparts morphing into giant pupae. The seats transmuting into eggs. The pupae began feeding on the corpses…the eggs hardening into stone sculptures. She gripped Echo's torso more firmly.

"Worry not," Echo said, "Dyscrasia is largely controlled now, thanks to Lord Lysis. He has reanimated Grave and controls him as he does the once-Queen. Instead of nurturing diseased elders, Grave has been turned toward raising humans. In his undeath, he is content."

Helen quietly stewed on the Doctor's status. She had known him to be a professor, not an enemy. Sorcery brought second lives to many, it seemed, including Bryhan. The Gray Lords and their supernatural companions had histories that were difficult to reconcile from her mortal perspective.

The smell of pine ceded to acrid smoke as they left the dense forest. In the distance upslope, over a dozen blackened towers stood eerily. The buildings had survived better than the numerous burnt trees surrounding the city. The vine-covered bricks were strangely more green than much of the desolation. Behind these, and higher still, were the colorful, mineral-rich zeniths of the Calx. The mountains had cradled the city of artisans. The group advanced on the rocky trail leading into the ash-laden district once known as Clan Tonn.

Navigating a craggy outcropping of rocks, they came upon an outer ring of mounded earth. It sloped upward to wrap ten evenly spaced bastions. Each fortification doubled as a furnace tower and was connected to the others by a continuous, although ruined, wall of stone.

"The city was built between the trees, needed for fuel, and the mines, in which ore was quarried. Colliers had maintained the earth mounds around this outer wall called Athanor Henge. These serpentine-shaped mounds doubled as soil kilns, covering wood as it kindled into charcoal. The lumber was sourced from the now-barren tree line marking the transition into mountainous terrain. Originally, the outer spires were made to separate metal from ore; these were the proper alchemical athanors and blast furnaces, and required the charcoal." Bryhan explained to Helen.

"It looks as if their fires burned the city and the surrounding forest," Helen said.

"In truth, the Clan had responsibly planted as many trees as they collected. Volcanic fallout caused the fires that ravaged this city. When Cypria's Gallwomb exploded, countless wildfires erupted across the Land." Echo reflected, "My birth was tumultuous for all."

Helen had already understood that Echo was born from Cypria's litter, but she hardly comprehended the scale of sorcery and the battle that transpired. The entire Land was still recovering. She peered through the many breaches in the outer wall called Athanor Henge. Brick buildings peppered the interior. Shadows flickered back and forth. Creeping fig vines blanketed the buildings. Tonn was indeed a ghost city.

Bryhan's face turned sullen.

Helen asked, "What are you looking at?"

"The ruins you see in color, I *see* in gray. Any color I do see is of things invisible to the living. I see pleasant memories in the ether: apple-red ghosts of my relatives, indigo apparitions of Grovel Tonn working the smithy, and ivory visages of Whitebeard harvesting medicinal herbs." He paused. "Golden yellow echoes of my mother's soul, Lady Aleece, riding horseback outside the Henge. My father Kaiyn was the Clanlord, but he turned to his elder son for his pride. My brother, Lordson Tyann. I never measured up to the expectations of royalty. It did not interest me either. As Tyann spent time being groomed for leadership, I spent time with my mother. As my clan fell apart at the climax of the Ill Age, my allegiance went quickly to the foundling Echo. In my final days of life, he became my reason for living. Past death, I serve him still."

Emboldened by her newfound access to information, Helen's curiosity ignited. "If your Gray powers went unchecked, would the world look the same to both living and dead?"

"Do you know about the power, beauty, and terror of the colored fires seen by the dead?" Echo asked his curious companion.

"I see the lack of color in your wounds, Lord." Helen noted the abundance of papyrus invitations roosting on rocks and ruins alike. "And tinted phantoms I have seen rise from Lysis' Pyre."

"That fire may be the only medium that both undead and living see in the same way." Echo could see several flags wave, torn and ruined by weather and age. The fading sigil of Bryhan's father eroded on these: a pair of rampant wyverns. Perhaps it was right that the sigil eroded, given that Clanlord Kaiyn never returned with his Legion. *Clan Tonn is all but erased. Outsiders crawl the mines, the forests, and the fortress. They are not all born from the Tonn family. However, they are its heirs.* If this were a simple scouting mission, then Bryhan and Echo would have stealthily entered through the numerous breaches in the

Henge. "Today, we enter by the main gate," Echo decided. "We will head to the City Commons."

Bryhan agreed, "Yes, Sharon deserves a formal entrance."

The main gate, a series of opened portcullises and hinged doors, each a curtain of scrolled, wrought iron ten yards tall, was open in welcome. Great beauty remained evident in the ruins; the cobblestone of the main thoroughfare was not the simple array of bricks Helen expected, but was instead a carpet of colored, patterned blocks inlaid with polished minerals and gilded ingots. The artisanship displayed here had been not practiced since the Ill Age.

Surprisingly, the gate was manned.

A soldier wearing a helmet with a conical snout peered down from the bastion. The man's extremities were armored, but his torso and legs were not. Raising the visor to reveal his face, the watchman, which Bryhan recognized as Kohl, shouted to the party.

"Hail, Clanlord Bryhan—" Kohl saluted him with gauntleted fists, then he ran down from the mezzanine to ground level. As a youngster Kohl had scavenged the mines for colored minerals for producing paint. Now his digging gauntlets were modified for battle, sporting lengthy talons of wrought iron.

"Good Kohl, I have long lost my sovereign flail, my brother, my father, my mother, and even my life. You need not address me by title any longer."

Lacking Bryhan's royal upbringing, the refugee replied with an improvised formality, "Ruhyn, Master of Joy, wants us to call you as such."

"Master Ruhyn is a good man to follow."

Behind Kohl, the buildings breathed through gaping windows—or so it seemed. Wind-borne phantoms worked their way from the mountaintops, rushing through alleys in pulsating gusts. The Tonn District was the only to have mastered glass and outfitted its windows with its luxurious beauty. Sadly, the clear panes were now all broken into jagged shards, adorning windowsills like broken teeth.

The buildings' disrepair amplified that of the streets too. In the corners and indents of grout lay films sparkling powder, broken bottles, and fractured ornaments. It may be haunted, but it remained a rich place. Time and decay could not take away its accumulated spirit. The Outsiders kept it kindling.

"Without 'r Master, we'd have no hope."

Echo said, "Indeed, Kohl. Please take us to Ruhyn. We have dark news."

"Aye. As does he." Kohl led the mounted guests on the main thoroughfare toward the inner ring of furnaces. He noticed Helen. "Where's Sharon?"

"She succumbed to illness," Echo said. "Curator Helena travels with us in her stead."

Distracted by a flock of Lysis' sprites flying overhead and dispersing into the City, Helen missed the introduction. Outsiders scattered away from them, seeking shadows.

Kohl said, "Don't be worrin' about them urchins lurkin' about, Miss Helena. Those 'r the people Ruhyn hopes to adopt. They come from afar. Clanless strays. Too suspicious to join the community still, but the Athanor ruins 'r safer than the forest. They're masking themselves with mud 'nstead of metal, trying to imitate our helms."

Helen saw one of mud-covered urchins standing just ahead, apart from the road. A magical sprite landed on his arm. Lysis' invitation mesmerized him. It hovered then beckoned for him to follow. The brilliant fairy tugged at his sleeves trying to lead him to the road.

"It is not a trap," Helen called. "You should go to the Keep."

Her voice startled him. He looked away from the magical parchment to see the woman who beckoned him. She rode a giant mantis! The boy ran terrified. The sprite disintegrated into ash.

The roadside was empty again. They moved forward in silence. Abandoned wagons littered the street. Rust-covered lampposts wrapped in vines stood erect, unlit. Hitching posts waited for horses that would never return. Racks with clothes near empty dyer vats were twisted, worn, and ash-laden. Helen felt sorry for a family of abandoned footwear, sitting obediently beside an open threshold: three sets of petrified leather boots. One moved suddenly, and a mouse escaped. How do the metal-proud folk feel about these ruins? Humans still survived here. There must be too few to repair it.

Before them splayed an arc of furnaces, encircling the City Commons like monoliths. Most of these towers were forges that gave artisans, like blacksmiths and glass blowers, the close access to fire they required. The party rounded a bend and finally saw into the foot of the Calx mountain. At its base, was an exhausted quarry, transformed into an amphitheater. The Commons was lined with shadow-filled arcades intersecting the towers, a string of ruined archways. This curvilinear edifice circumvented the quarry. Three forge towers stood as sanctuaries for rooks. Once, the smoking stacks would have coughed noxious clouds to repel the scavenger birds. Concentric, tiered steps led from the city, through exquisite, relief-carved colonnades, each decorated with a parade figures chronicling Clan's heroic tales. These pillars led the party downward to the eerily empty arena. Opposite the steps, double metal doors were inset into the mountain: the Tonn Mine and Tomb entrance. The threshold had been recently barricaded with three toppled pillars, hastily felled.

Echo and Bryhan silently read the memories here. The spirit world was dominated by the Spring Courting Contest. Men had vied for young women, who would stand atop mammoth slabs in the amphitheater's center. Here, in turn, the maidens would call out challenges. Sometimes, a woman would demand a brave, skilled warrior to fight an impromptu tournament. Others demanded to be entertained, and only a witty, comedic man could win a heart then. Cruel women chose this time to embarrass suitors already committed to them, luring them into a public trial highlighting their weaknesses. The specificity of the contests were not announced prior to the Contest, the maidens keeping their desires secret. The anticipation often maddened contestants, since eligible men were gullible and subject to the dramatic impulses of youth. The outcomes were not binding by law, except when the royal family participated. Bryhan's mother Aleece had challenged a champion to kill a pair of white serpents plaguing the miners. Kaiyn answered. He climbed the great stones, knelt, kissed her hand, and accepted the trial. Then he left for the mines alone and returned one day later with two slaughtered wyverns. His sigil was thus born and the ivory scales saved for his future Sons' armor.

Hovering over them on the mountainside was the inner citadel. It loomed over the Commons. Set in its walls were intricate stained glass murals, faceted with countless transparent jewels, chronicling ancient legends. Byproducts of the copper refining furnaces produced its brilliant blue and green insets. Beyond that, Apothecary Whitebeard's tower stood, and a flood of memories flowed forth in the astral realm, stirring Son Bryhan's emotions.

Bryhan noticed tendrils of smoke rising ahead. "It must be a fine day if your men are working metal again. Grovel Tonn's forge burns again. Perhaps Master Ruhyn is indeed bringing back the finer aspects of civilization."

"You have that wrong. This fire will disappoint."

A hundred yards away, twenty men huddled in front of the active forge. They donned ceremonial helmets resembling animal heads. Whereas Kohl's helm had resembled a hound, the others featured horns, antlers, and manes. Master Ruhyn was prominent from Helen's view. He was without doubt the tallest of the group. His barrel chest was the widest. His ornamented, tiger-themed helm had unique parts: the faceless bascinet had a hauberk mane, bordered with feline hide, and saber teeth extended over his ears to frame the last component: a lacquered mask, white with purple stripes. Beneath dirt, his body was decorated in burn scars, both intentional branding and unintended wounds.

Helen scrutinized Master Ruhyn. "He doesn't seem joyful."

Guard Bryhan explained, "He laughs sometimes, but solemnly. The Outsiders gather to him since they believe in his vision that joy can be brought back."

"Clanlord Bryhan Tonn, welcome," Master Ruhyn said. "I would be expectin' you to have arrived via your normal route, but am gladdened to see tradition honored."

As with any healthy human, Ruhyn's aura burned red as his blood. But he was a nuanced fellow. Echo marveled at the green, astral plumes billowing from Ruhyn's mouth with each exhalation. This was how the man's glass blowing skills manifested in the astral world: it was if he breathed flames.

Behind, stood his masked captains. Like a cadre of mythological beasts they cantered about a fire. Most had forgotten their true names, or intentionally shed them over the years, as they survived the Ill Age without parents. The canine-masked Kohl took his place amongst his fellow captains. Mark held his iron pontil, the glass-blowing shaft now served as a blunt mace. His visorless, barbute helm was mantled with bear fur.

Then there was the satyr-like man, Burden, with muscular legs bowed like a goat. His feet seemed to be always seeking out rocks to balance on. He was an immense character, with a hammer in one hand and pick in the other. As a teen he had gathered and broken raw ore from the quarries, making it digestible by the fires. Familiar with the animals of the Calx, his helmet sprouted four curled ram horns.

Dismounting his insectan steed, Guard Bryhan announced, "Hail, Master Ruhyn. We came because we must perform a funeral in the mines, to bury—"

"—burnin', my Clanlord. We're burnin' here. Not buryin' anymore," interrupted the mud covered Ruhyn, bracing himself against his iron blowpipe, a makeshift weapon originally used by his deceased forefathers to inflate molten glass.

A luminescent sprite landed on the pipe. It roosted on his bar and beckoned him. Ruhyn swatted it. Helen gasped as the paper creature crumbled. How confident he must be to disregard Lord Lysis' invitation? Helen thought. His weapon was more valuable to him than some magical fairy. Now its pipe spun in his palm, churning as did his mind, releasing the faint scent of its beeswax coating.

They stood within the shadows of the inner towers. All, save one, were cold. A singular furnace breathed fire, one of the outer ring. Clouds of burnt flesh exhaled from its stack.

"You have used Grovel's forge for cremation?" Guardian Bryhan realized.

"Just this instance, Son Bryhan. We're preferrin' to use the catacombs. The tunnels 're no longer safe. Our abandoned forges are now a temple for 'r dead," Ruhyn explained. He sighed as he gathered his thoughts. "These 'r the remains of the creature escaping the mines. We slew 'em at great cost."

"Devils," Burden declared. His breath carried the sweet

scent of smoked lavender.

All turned their attention to the hybrid carcasses, a heap of exoskeletons and vertebrates. They had torsos and heads like humans, atop thorax and abdomens of insects.

"Chromanti," Foundling Echo identified the creatures, looking over Bryhan's shoulder.

"Beasts being a mix of man 'n elder. The mines 'r infested with 'em," Ruhyn assented.

Helen thought it strange that they did not seem to acknowledge the irony: they feared the hybrids, and they preferred to maintain distance from the Keep. Yet they dressed themselves like hybrid beasts. Half human, half creature.

Ruhyn shifted his stance, appearing uncomfortable. He leaned on his blowpipe for support. His armor moved, revealing a bleeding ribcage.

It was then that Echo saw that Master Ruhyn was injured. "You are hurt!" The Outsiders were not accepting of the Grays' sorcery, but they were open to humans like Sharon touching them. Echo turned his head to his nurse, "Helena, please go to him."

Helen dismounted and stumbled forward as her legs became reacquainted with the ground. She balanced herself by extending her black forearms, drawing attention to her unnaturally curled nails. The band of men looked at her hands curiously. She wished she had a mask to cover her face. Without it, it was open for scrutiny. She shrank away from the silent, blank looks that undoubtedly glared from behind visors, her confidence shaken.

"Who's she?" Ruhyn asked.

"Our new curator, Helena. As you inform us about what transpired here, she can heal you. Are you still in danger?"

Ruhyn held out a hand indicating Helen to come no further. The hasty rejection deflated whatever confidence she had gained from Echo's introduction.

"No disrespectin' meant, but healing me is best done after we tend to those who passed. My wounds aren't fatal." Eventually he muttered, "We're safe here in the city. All attacks bein' underground. Many men died in the mines. Had to seal it off. Now we're burn'n ten captains," Ruhyn said. The survivors stared at the raging fire.

"Sharon would want to burn with them," Echo said. "It is the primary reason we came here. The situation is not as I predicted. I too prefer her entombed below in the mountains. Her friends will reduce to ash, and so will she."

The Master assented. Bryhan laid her body down so that all could pay their last respects. One by one, the masked men kneeled, bowed, and lay a hand on Sharon's head. Ruhyn trailed after his men. Echo signaled to Helen with a nod. Helen walked forward and whispered farewell into Sharon's ear. Echo followed close behind. Then Bryhan lifted Sharon and strode toward the furnace opening, laying her to rest in cinders.

Behind Helen were the empty masks of the fallen, propped atop iron stanchions, looking toward their bodies inside the forge. Helen stared at Sharon's burning husk. She held onto her braid tied with Sharon's ribbon. They had outlived a fire when they first met. They had found their way to the Keep together. Death chased them, failed to catch them, until now.

Echo and Bryhan saw things differently. They knew her body was done already, and knew that her soul lived on. They viewed the ceremony as marking a transition already passed. Now they saw white and grey flames cushioning Sharon's orange ghost as she navigated the ashen debris of the oven, joining the circle of her burning friends' spirits. Her spirit was not harmed in the fire, and her body was decaying anyway. She was not unhappy in her death either. Still, Echo felt responsible for it. He remembered her healing him when she was younger. He had not asked for her help. He was in Grave's Theater, and she wandered in and she instantly connected with him, similar to how Bryhan had instinctively protected him in the Ill Age. Some intuitively found their purpose. He wished he had their conviction. Perhaps that was a trait reserved for humans.

As if in honor of the dead, a flock of fluttering paper sprites perched atop the masks. As the birds flapped their magical wings, the edges kindled and glowed. Burden alone had no cranes roosting on him, indicating his genuine courage and stubbornness. All the other men had sprites perched loosely to their shoulders. But these went as unnoticed as the presence of flies.

After a reverent time passed, the group dispersed. Helen began examining the men. Ruhyn had a gash in his abdomen and fared the worst. He sat silently as she cleansed his side, digesting the news of Sharon's demise. Helen's delicate, blackened fingers soothed his pain as they caressed his skin, removing soil from the wound. Her presence was hypnotic. She prepared the wound with her oils and thyme. Even as he sorrowed, Ruhyn was warmed by Helen's touch. She inked inverted chevrons, horizontal and vertical bars. She concealed her art then with ribbons of fabric.

The Master of Joy had no intention of going to the Keep for protection, but perhaps Clanlord Bryhan could help them here. Determined that it was time to convey what evidence they had of their mysterious enemy, he ordered, "Kohl, show 'em the horn."

Kohl dug through the pile with his gauntlets, retrieving a curved elephantine tusk. It was from an eldritch soldier, like the one Bryhan rode. The center was hollowed out. The tip polished. He presented it to Ruhyn.

Echo inspected it. "It is a calling horn. Given the size and behavior of those you killed, they must have been scouts. They are looking for something and mean to call others once they have it."

Several of the Tonn men grunted. One said, "It released screamin' banshees. Terrible and out o' tune—"

"For your ears, maybe," Echo interrupted. "But to your enemy, I am sure it sounded clear. More await somewhere to follow its cries." He looked past the clarion horn to focus on the ghosts rising from the chromanti carcasses. Hovering above them, his own face took shape. Then three tiny eyes materialized between the two. Ocelli. Dark rimmed. Angled inquisitively. Reflective, like glass. The ghostly black orbs looked into his own soul. A wet mouth beneath the eyes smiled. The cloudy apparition was difficult to discern, being of a translucent white ether that contrasted poorly with the grey physical world. An invisible fog rolled in from behind him, urging him forward. Multiple hands of mist tugged at him. He could not pry his eyes away. He took a step toward the apparition. He was being lured by the spirit, but assumed he was in control over his senses, and was captivated. A woman hybrid. He determined to identify her. She seemed familiar, but every time he focused on her face, the vision altered...

Helen saw Echo's antennae twitching. She alerted Bryhan with a tap and a nod. The guard could not see the ether as well as Echo, but he sensed that his master was being hypnotized. He pulled Echo back from the offal, and the spell broke without any of the humans knowing that the spirits had reached out to him. Then, the chitinous carnage shifted, as would a spent fire settling. Real sparks shot forth, and fizzled. Bryhan ushered Echo further away, and the energetic flares subsided.

The men did not seem alarmed, though Helen was prepared to dismiss healing the men to attend her lord. For now Guard Bryhan seemed to be nonplused, so she continued. The Outsiders were all covered in the same white gore that had sprayed upon Echo three days ago.

"Will you come to the Keep for protection?" Bryhan asked.

"We still love our home. Your home," Ruhyn declined. "I return the invitation, not that a Clanlord requires it. Whenever you serve out your duty to Echo, you are welcome here."

Guard Bryhan said, "I understand, friend. You do not accept my death, or the fall of the Clan. And you distrust the

Keep. The danger here has never been more severe. Lysis commands the sprites to find yearning souls, and they continually go to you. You attract them because you feel insecure. Why deny this?"

"Tonn's royalty will be restored," the Master of Joy affirmed.

Burden grew anxious, knowing that Ruhyn's soul was being scrutinized. His own was thus exposed. "Clean spirits," he grunted, exchanging his weapons for a bundle of lavender and sage, which he ignited. All watched the ram-horned Outsider wave the smoldering brand around all the humans: Ruhyn, himself, and even Helen.

The smoke made Helen cough, and she gave a pleading look toward Echo.

"Burden is not much for usin' words," Ruhyn explained. "His smudging won't hurt you. We here trust in the powers of fire."

Echo could see the process dampen the white glow of the dead hybrids. Smudging worked better than Ruhyn knew.

Captain Burden whispered a single word as a prayer, then extinguished the smoldering bundle on his skin. Physical pain often buries emotional woes; smoke was certainly not enough, Helen thought.

"We live here. We expect to die here." Ruhyn spoke for his men. "Your Lysis is welcome to come here. He could clear the mines better than us." He pointed to the mine entrance. "We sealed the tunnels when we retreated. Not just the main gate here in the Commons, but all the cave entrances," Ruhyn pointed to many spots in the pockmarked terrain.

They all watched Echo survey the mountains. Only he could spy ether miles away. They had not closed all the thresholds. There was an opening in one. There, white fire flared like a distant star. From within, a hybrid crawled out, following a ribbon of ether. Echo traced the invisible fibers radiating from the hole: from the crag-ridden mountainside, over ramps of scree, through the timberline, into the circle of athanors, and down into the city center, working their way toward them. Comprising hundreds of miniature, ethereal hybrids, the astral threads hovered over the ground.

The others watched how Echo's head followed an invisible trail from the mountains to the pile of dead creatures at their feet. They could not see the translucent tendrils worming into the chromanti remains, each translucent and glowing white as was the haunting woman's face. Her face formed again. White, fiery worms wriggled from her mouth, undulating toward Echo. This energy awakened the dead hybrids beneath. A severed torso began crawling toward Echo following the magical ropes, reaching for them with unbalanced hands.

"Clanlord Bryhan!" Ruhyn alerted. "Watch out!"

Bryhan pierced the animated gore with his spear, and then stepped on the worming remains. Ghostly tendrils suddenly spat. Echo's sorcerous net had been cast wide to search for the hybrids afar. It found and agitated the flesh nearby instead.

Burden came forward with his hammer and pick to assist but before he could strike, a call from the mountains froze him in his tracks: *Wwwuuuurrrr! Wurrrrr!*

Echo pointed toward the breach in the caves. "Prepare your men. The chromanti have just breached your blockades!"

All the Outsiders began shouting:

"They're comin' from the caves!"

"They've broken the seals!"

"There is movement behind the glass walls of the Great Hall!"

Wwwuuuurrrr!

Helen glanced at the rocky slopes to witness streams of colossal human-locusts.

"To battle!" Ruhyn yelled. His men spread out.

Echo commanded, "Helen, get to the nearest furnace. Light the warning brand. Hide in one of the cold forges."

"But?" Helen pleaded for more information. How did the enemy advance so quickly?

Bryhan urged, "Hide now!" Then he was off.

She ran toward a ruined tower. In her peripheral vision, she saw chaos. Several arrows whizzed past. Flashes of fire, bolts of electricity. Was Echo using sorcery? Clinking of metal, death throes, horn calls…

Captain Mark sprinted toward the colonnades to gain a better vantage, only to be abruptly met by the enemy. Three wailing female hybrids crested the Common's rim. His pontil rod lifted immediately to affix the forerunner through its human torso, but then the weapon and he were lost as the beast fell, crushing him. Three more enemies hurdled into this carnage.

Burden strode up the amphitheater staircase toward these multiple opponents. He threw his pick toward one, and whilst that weapon flew, he advanced on a second that reared on two of its hind legs. Rolling, he ducked beneath the reach of the flailing upper limbs, lashing his hammer on the anchored legs. These snapped, and the hybrid toppled. The third moved fast, leaning down to grab Burden's legs with its human arms. This chromantaur was then gored by the tusks of Bryhan's soldier ant, which lifted it into the air and away. Burden gained his footing, retrieved his pick, and rejoined the melee.

Meanwhile, Helen dodged falling bodies to arrive at the burning furnace. She threw Lysis' brand into the crematorium. Instantly, lemon flames and blue flares spat, and the funerary fire turned into brilliant colors. "Lord Lysis, I pray you come with god speed," Helen said, and the satellite pyre called to its parent. Then, she retreated directly to a cold, deserted forge.

Ruhyn dipped the far end of his pipe into the fire to collect flames, and blew in the opposite hole to billow them. Then he loaded it with feathered darts. These missiles ignited as they launched toward the eyes of two encroaching chromanti. Blinded and enflamed, the hybrids curled up, incapacitated.

Kohl managed to mount the back of another. He dug his gauntlets into the vulnerable sides of his new mount. His arms were drenched with cold ichor.

Helen was momentarily safe in a pile of cool ash. She caught her breath as she peered through the slats of the iron door. Humans and Bryhan's soldier ant battled against hybrid versions of them. Echo darted one way, and Bryhan followed. She saw an Outsider surrounded by four hulking chromanti. Then a fifth came, and the five formed a star formation, tugging on the mudman's head and limbs so tightly as to levitate the body, until ligaments failed and sinew stretched beyond measure. The right leg separated. Helen looked away. She attempted to nibble her fingernails to allay her anxiety, but her hands shook too much. Then nausea clouded her thoughts, so she used her hands to steady herself.

The dissonant ringing of metal ceded to the tortuous, resistant screams of men as they were stretched between opposing chromanti. There were scores of hybrids crawling up every hill, furnace and chimney, and there were no more Outsiders walking freely. Where was Lord Echo? Helen could see several clusters. Groups of enemies encircled their targets. Six, she counted. Like the pattern on their chests.

There she saw Echo cornered by several chromanti. His wings spread open as he assumed his fighting stance, rearing on his hind legs. The exposed white and pink undersides issued a mordant warning. His enemies approached cautiously. If only his wings could fly him to safety, but even if not frayed from battle they could not sustain a long flight. Echo lashed out with his arms. He missed their bodies, but must have damaged their auras. Three retreated, wailing in agony.

Bryhan suddenly obscured her view, his scaled armor a blur. He pushed, struck, and swatted with his metal spear. He gored the exposed back of one beast that faced Lord Echo, his weapon lodged temporarily beside the opponent's spine. He leaned onto the opposite end to lever the impaled creature into the path of another. The two collapsed into a heap. His spear freed, he fluidly blocked a strike to his right side, rotated while stepping toward another opponent, slashed at a hybrid's knee rendering the leg a twisted ruin, turned again to strike another.

Chaos ruled the Commons. The reluctant mud-masked boys were forced into action. Some had been retreating, only to find themselves cornered. Makeshift cudgels shook in trembling hands. Given years of peace, they would have joined Ruhyn's community. They would have outgrown their reclusiveness. Instead, death was thrust upon them today. Like fledglings thrown from a nest, they died fast. They fought on the same battlefield as Ruhyn's men—but individually. They were torn asunder one by one.

Helen's eyes welled. She witnessed the carnage while hidden, imbibing many raging emotions: hate, urgency, pain, fear. Her heart dropped into her stomach. Within days of finding a purposeful role, she had to watch her group's destruction. Her freedom from the Keep, her promising future, was being taken from her.

Creamy *lapis elixir* sprayed the scene, as did red blood and gray ash.

"Save the Clanlord!" Ruhyn rallied his helmeted captains. He issued burning darts until his pipe was grabbed by several hands.

Burden went berserk, his pick cracking carapaces and crippling enemies. He did not stop to finish his kills, but moved from creature to creature like a whirlwind, the momentum of his heavy weapons carrying him from target to target.

The enemy came in large numbers. Her view became congested with bodies. Occasional blades broke through, as did several human cries. Then the mass broke into multiple clusters. In moments, her companions were encased in separate mounds of coalesced chromanti. Ruhyn. Bryhan. Echo. Four others. All arrested and splayed into star shapes. Lord Echo could not escape. Six more chromanti, backing into the openings between those who held him, and then plumes of chemicals sprayed onto her Lord. The fog blurred the scene.

Helen compulsively searched her hair for Sharon's ribbon to console herself. Her trusted muse was ineffective. *Sharon, I will join you sooner than I had imagined.* Helen had to search beyond her familiar muses for options, but there was no time to ruminate. Her primal instincts knew that staying hidden was unacceptable. Staying still would drown her in despair. Duty called. She was compelled to move, but did so out of panic. She was no warrior, but fate lured her into a battle.

She darted from her hiding place, jumped over a canine-shaped helmet that concealed the identity of the decapitated head therein, hastily approached the ring of enemy encircling her Gray Lord, sprang upon the nearest enemy and draped her flag over its head. Her nails broke as they pried into its soft eyes.

She had caught the hybrid unaware. It was blinded for sure. Before she could engage another she was struck on the head by its flailing arms. She flew, the skull of her forehead bare, her flag clutched in her left hand. Her head banged onto rock. She lay upon her back, chest throbbing. She could see the blinding sun, but its rays were being blocked by an enormous shadow. A storm?

Then, about the ascending column of magical smoke, she espied a larger black cloud rolling in with tornadic splendor. Within was the visage of an angelic warrior: Lord Lysis. Several legions of winged insects carried his form alone, countless flickering sprite-like wasps suspended him in the air. Lysis' cloud descended the same instant it arrived. Wind raced in tumultuous currents, as if the Sky had emptied its lungs. Stirred ash concealed all and bit into all unarmored skin. Each chromantaur was overrun with wasps, roaches, and flies. *Eviscamir* carved holes in the Sky and Land, arcs of lightening flashed where it slashed, and white gore sank in its wake.

Helen could not sit upright to witness all the madness. She could hear nothing over the sound of her ringing ears, but she felt the ground quake as if the Calx range had avalanched. Bloody bodies reeking of chromantaur ichor fell around her. Helen could not move away. She shook and reverberated with the collapsing of furnace towers.

Between the limbs of the dead that blanketed her, she saw the silhouette of Lord Lysis, though Helen had no idea how he arrived. Then a moment of odd beauty enthralled her. As the hybrids attempted to engage Lysis, his sorcery drained the color from their groping hands. A tug-of-war over hue ensued across the ether. He depleted them of life force, glowing brighter as his adversaries turned to gray, fell to ash, and blew away.

Blood flowed over Helen's eyes. All turned dark. Some time passed as she was carried away. Sight gone now, she could only hear. Her flag was taken from her hand and wrapped about her head. She was lifted in her Lord's arms, and she rested dreamily. Echo knew she could not see or read ether, so he spoke aloud to the Lysis. "I survive. As does my brave Helena."

To his fellow Lord, Echo mind spoke, *"It is as the once-Queen had indicated. I am their target, I know this because they handled me carefully. They want me alive."*

"The interrogations supported the once-Queen's suspicions. I have been tracking you since my minions discovered white blood in Tonn. Helen's beacon confirmed the worst and guided me to you. Your healer needs healing herself." Lysis commanded, *"I sense a great army streaming into the Land. To the Keep now!"*

III: Desecrating the Underworld Hollow

A PIERCING STRIKE FROM a chromantaur lance had delivered a puncture wound to Burden's shoulder, tearing the flesh as it exited. Hasty cauterizations sealed it, enabling him to retain blood while being transported from Tonn Commons to the Chromlechon Keep. He fainted anyway before the masses of Lysis' insects levitated him. He stayed incoherent until after they landed.

On South Gate's solid ground, Burden regained some awareness. He defied being handled by any more of the Grays or Keepers, and remained in a slump against the parapet away from them. Ruhyn was more accepting of their hosts. Both needed time to recover from the surreal flight. They stayed in the courtyard for a time, until the Master determined that his Captain's wounds, although not fatal, should not be ignored.

"Clanlord Bryhan, can you lead us to Helen? Capt'n

Burden's shoulder needs mendin' I believe."

"She is inside the Keep, in the Operating Theater. This way." Bryhan helped Ruyhn carry the heavy man through dank corridors reminiscent of Tonn's upper mines. Upon arrival, Ruhyn brought his friend closer to Echo, Grave, and Lysis who surrounded the central table. Helen lay unconscious, her head wrapped in bandages.

Burden moaned, eyes half shut beneath his helm. "Healer?"

"Helen recovers from being operated on herself." Echo explained, "Doctor Grave can work on you."

"Yes Lord, I will minister to—," Grave stopped himself short. The Outsider's aura was riddled with fearful perceptions of the Doctor.

Had Burden been healthy, he may have been able to control his reflexes. He may have been able to reconcile that Lord Lysis had long since owned the golem doctor. Lysis had not destroyed all his enemies and eldritch foes; instead he had assumed control over their bodies. And there was evidence that the Gray Powers were used wisely, since even Clan Tonn's noble Son Bryhan, reanimated by Echo, was in the room now partnering with Doctor Grave. There was no denying, however, that the Doctor had once haunted Tonn, collecting their mothers and sacrificing them to the eldritch gods. Twenty years of living with the consequences of those acts only amplified Burden's distrust.

"Devil!" Burden recognized the demon, freshly blood-ied from operating. "Butcher!"

Regardless, Doctor Grave advanced with a vial of odiferous salts.

Lysis halted him. "Grave, stop. Remain focused on Echo's curator."

"I merely planned on sedating him. But as you command, my Lord."

Lysis turned to Ruhyn, "Your man's wounds are not severe, but will get worse the more he flails. Take him out."

Ruhyn contained his frothing friend and exited toward the tunnels. Away from the Grays, in the comfort of a stone corridor, Burden eventually calmed. Clearly, they would have to wait until Helen was able to cure again.

Meanwhile, within the Theater, Grave completed sewing Helen's left eyelid into the recess of its ocular cavity. Her right eye was swollen shut, purple all around. After cleansing the skin, he padded the vacated side with gauze and used the washed remains of her flag as an additional bandage.

Echo asked Grave, "Your prognosis?"

"Her forehead had been clawed. It is fortuitous that she was collected before she bled out. She is stabilized, but will need time to recover." Grave arranged his operating utensils. "Another replacement ceremony is in order."

Echo was quiet. Helen had just begun her service to him. It was not right to have her replaced already. Knowing that he was the target of the enemy's hunt affected him greatly. Countless dead were left unburied in Tonn. Yet he had no solution to the madness.

The Doctor looked dispassionately toward Echo,

mistaking the latter's silence for approval. "I will gather the initiates."

Lysis interjected, "Grave, Foundling Echo did not order another curator."

"Helena will keep her position," Echo confirmed. The Doctor contained his disapproval with a stifled sigh and commenced cleaning the table.

Lysis communicated to his fellow Gray, *"You are not responsible for the harm they caused."*

"These hybrids look like me."

"Despite what you think, you are not one of them."

"I am not human. And the hybrids hunt me. Where do I belong?"

Lysis grabbed his shoulder, *"With us."*

Doctor Grave extended a small bowl to Bryhan. Helen's left eye lay therein. "This belongs to his curer. Shall I dispose of it?"

"Nay," Bryhan considered how he had dealt with his own artificial arm. "I will return it to her. She deserves to decide." Bryhan accepted the container. He procured a pouch from the Doctor, and wrapping the eyes in gauze, stored it within. "Does she know yet?"

"She has not awakened yet for anyone to tell her, and I doubt her memory is sharp enough to remember the attack. The damaged right eye remains in place. If it functions, it will likely provide distorted vision. Only time will tell. You can inform her of her condition when she rouses." Grave spooled up his stitching threads and sheathed his sewing needles.

Lysis spoke openly through the ether, *"Something in the ether is off, but I cannot determine the source. Assess her spirit."*

Grave interjected, *"Her aura maybe taxed, but I see no contagion like the previous healer had."*

"Lord, I will look closer," Echo offered. Blessed with the finest sight among the Grays, he examined Helena's aura. A celestial cloud of tiny stars hovered over her head. Each spark was a nucleus of six miniature hybrids, their abdomens outfaced, heads centered, jawing away on her life force. Like masses of ticks, they adhered to her psyche. The feline shade of her pelt largely maintained its green glow while scratching relentlessly. Grave had removed most of the poisonous ichor, but its phantasmal residue was plain to see for Echo. Helena's mind now associated the iconic shape of the sun with fear. The feline familiar's fur faded to gray wisps wherever the hybrid masses localized. Consistent with her mind's associations, the hybrid sorcery fed on her soul. *These hybrids feed on the intangible as we do,* considered Echo. *Can they work it too as we do?*

Echo worked Helena's shade with his antennae. With a graceful arcane gesture, his arms cut the air, and the astral parasites were excised. In a short time, her soul was cleansed. Yet the ghosts respawned slowly. Looking closely, he discerned ropes emerging from Helen's halo. His antennae combed the ethereal mists for the ends of those chains, homing in on a dense phosphorous veil. Wherever he searched, the mist followed. Then it dawned on him. It was not following his appendages. It was coming *from* them. It was if the essence of his white blood was subliming through his shell.

Echo had suffered many deep cuts, but the enemy had taken care not to divide him as they did the urchins and Ruhyn's captains. In Helen's absence, Doctor Grave had attended to his physical wounds. The superficial slices to his wrists and legs were sealed. Yet the contagion was bound to him.

"Lord, Helen's spirit is fine. But there are strange entities in the astral realm attached to me." Echo explained, *"They reflect the horrors to come. Thousands of them. I am corrupted. My presence threatens her...you—"*

"You are not a threat to me, Echo. Your curator can clean the mist from your soul," said Lysis.

"I fear that she cannot. When she tries, they...she...it... will likely spread to her."

Lysis ascertained that Echo saw more in this mist, *"Grave may be able to do something while Helen recovers."*

"I am not so sure, Lord." The Doctor looked perplexed. *"I cannot remedy what I cannot detect."*

Echo said, *"Lysis, I am surprised you sensed the markings at all. Even so, I am sure you do not see them...her...as I do."* Echo picked at his waist, where it transitioned from soft flesh to hard chitin. Softened from travel, and scraped from battle, portions began to flake. How long could he hold off molting?

"If you have been marked, we can mislead them. I will need a sample of your shell." Lysis drew *Ferrus Eviscamir* and carefully extracted a delaminating section from Echo's middle right leg. Grave understood what was necessary, and assisted

in sloughing off the infected chitin. Echo looked in horror as the shell fragment released sentient steam: five-eyed visages of a mantis-woman filled his vision. The Foundling confirmed to them that it was sufficiently tainted, since only he could see the witch's white faces bound to it. Echo could not pull his gaze away until Lysis ordered the Doctor to take it out of sight, to prepare it for further crafting.

The skeletal lord could not see the hybrid infection, but he did connect with it as he held the skin. Lysis' mind reached miles via an ethereal web connecting him to every creature he had reanimated. Through this network, Lysis sensed what his minions observed. A celestial map, composed of his minions, came into focus. From the Gorgepath, they were extinguished under a rolling dark tide.

Lysis raised *Eviscamir* suddenly.

Bryhan gripped his spear in readiness, awaiting the Lord's explanation.

"The hybrid army comes, so communicates my Horde. Thousands approach the Keep."

Boonnnngg. Booongg. From afar, a chorus of alarms rang to punctuate Lysis' alert.

Grave inquired, "Lord, there has been no army besides ours for twenty years. Where could such an army have been hiding?"

"Doctor, you may learn from their corpses after I end them."

"Do they come for Echo?" asked Bryhan.

The Gray Foundling affirmed, "It seems they do."

Grave added, "An army threatens all."

"They will not get to Echo, let alone enter the Keep," Lysis declared. He turned to the Doctor. "Echo must be kept isolated as much as possible. Grave, take them to the most remote place within the Keep: the Underworld Hollow."

"That is hallowed ground!" It was sacred to Grave. It had not been utilized since the once-Queen crafted the golems from the earth; it was his birthplace. The Doctor considered many alternative locations, including the collapsed nurseries where he and other golems had brought elder larvae out of eggs. Most were near the surface and difficult to defend. Grave held his tongue and relented to Lysis' stare. "With haste, my Lord."

"Escort Echo and his party there immediately. On your way back, bring me a chromantaur from your dungeon. Use the skin sample to disguise it. Meet me upon South Gate's parapets as I mobilize the Keep's defenses."

To Echo, he asserted, *"We will drive these hybrids back. I will handle whatever comes from outside the Keep, while you control whatever ails you."*

Lysis issued hundreds of commands as he strode to the surface. The honeycombed Chromlechon was abuzz with commotion. Each Gate was sealed. Larvalwyrmen wormed their way through the earth. Keepers ran with alarm torches that billowed clouds of sulfide, signaling that all should hide.

With no time to waste, Grave made to awaken Helen. He procured a jar of white crystals. "We cannot wait for her to awaken naturally. These ammoniac salts will wake her."

Doctor Grave unlatched the cover to his jar. Scents

emerged. The undead saw tendrils rope about her nightmare of battle, drag them back to into the confines of her head.

She jerked upright, into complete darkness. She squirmed violently, swatting the air and trying to tear off the bandages. Bryhan embraced her until she settled.

"Helena, your spirit is scarred from the battle. Do not worry. You are not alone." Echo spoke to her.

Breathing heavily she said, "I cannot move. Nor see."

Echo touched her shoulder with his antennae. "You have been injured. Your head is covered and must remain so. I am sorry, but we must move now."

Bryhan relaxed his hold to let her get off the table. She lost her balance and fell. He caught her.

"I will carry her," the Foundling said. Echo kneeled, and Bryhan and Grave raised Helen's weak body onto his thorax. Bryhan followed his Gray ensuring Helen remained as Echo stood.

In the tunnel, Ruhyn and Burden waited. They had come to the Keep reluctantly. Lysis' sorcery had saved them, but also demolished the Commons. Their city was pulverized and infested with hybrids. Ruhyn spun his blowpipe nervously. The men stared, silently examining the dancing shadows of torchlight. The Keep's tunnels were not unlike the mines to which they were accustomed. It was easy to imagine hybrids invading the corridor. Then the gong sounded again…

Boonnnngg.

Ruhyn rose to attention to greet Lord Echo, Helen, and Bryhan, "Clanlord Bryhan, what do the sounds mean?"

"They are alarms. The chromanti come. You are welcome to come with us, stay here, or go back to Tonn."

"Where do you go?"

"We go to hide the Gray Foundling. Helen is recovering, but we must withdraw," Bryhan said. Ryhun and Burden wanted to stay as close as they could to their Clanlord, but were not anxious to travel with Grave. The undead Guard read the humans' fears. "Doctor Grave will escort us to the destination. He will then depart."

"Then by your side, Clanlord, we go," Ruhyn said.

G RAVE LED THE group with an oil lantern. Echo followed in line, Helen resting on his back slowly regaining awareness. Then Bryhan came. Burden and Ruhyn trailed the party, maintaining some distance between themselves and the golem.

Echo had been scratching his skin, trying to scrape away both the itch and the haunting ghosts. His curer's fingers assessed his flesh and chitin as she held on. "Your skin is not right. It feels bruised and dirty. Smells of blood. I need to attend to you."

Echo continued walking at a brisk pace. "In due time, Helena. We must reach our destination first."

"After you care for your master, Captain Burden could use your skills too," Ruhyn added.

"I can try to help you now, but I cannot even see you. How long must I wear these bandages?"

Now was not time to explain her condition. Echo formulated an appropriate response, "Helena, we are all injured to some degree. We must keep moving. We can rest and check our wounds after we reach the Hollow."

They trudged the sandy walkways of the Keep's lower levels for an hour. Grave led the party deep into the Keep's core. "The dungeon is just up ahead."

"Dungeon?" Burden whispered to Ruhyn, limping along and carrying his pick as best his weary body could.

"Burden, 'tis not our destination. We just passin' through."

"You do not trust me, yet you follow?" Doctor Grave scoffed, "Lord Lysis instructed me to take you to the once-Queen's vault, which I do. After, I must depart to organize the Keep's defenses. So be delighted that you will be rid of me soon enough."

Helen grew increasingly uncomfortable and frustrated. Here she was in her home grounds, but she was not being permitted to walk. Rather, she was being carted through like baggage. Helen's blindness did not diminish her familiarity with the earth. She had grown to know and seek comfort within the Keep's cavernous belly. She often would roam in complete darkness in the tunnels she had already explored. She knew the stone textures intimately: how they felt a day after rain had fallen, since it would eventually seep its way down and wet the walls; how they felt the deeper one descended, ever more natural and less sculpted. She urged to touch stone.

Instead, she touched her master looking for bruises.

An angry voice inside the Gray's head lashed out: *She must let me go...let me out...* His antennae shook. He fought to find the source of the entity, and control it. It suddenly dissipated. "Helena, my skin is sore. Please wait till we rest to inspect it further."

Confused and rejected, Helen forced herself to remain as still as possible to avoid irritating her Lord. She was lulled into a daze recalling her time here. She had squirreled away all sorts of curios, beneath studios, cellars, in crawlways, and under bedrock. Many would not regard them as treasures if found, actually; they were not gilded ornaments but were just interestingly shaped stones, curiously warped insect carcasses, or scraps of art projects left to decay in the lower studios. She had often gotten lost as she explored, either looking for new items to collect or looking for old caches. Deep in the bowels of the earth she roamed in darkness. Faint sounds of the other Keepers would reach her, but their sources could not be trusted; sound bounced irregular, redirecting itself too much. Before panic would ever set in, one of Lysis' glowing sprites would appear. Lord Lysis may terrify her, but his minions comforted her often. Hence, Helen held fast to a faith that his furies would show her the way in darkness. As they had before in the Keep. As one led her here twenty years ago.

She had learned caving skills on her sorties. These evolved into instincts. For instance, walking became an advanced form of crawling. Before every step, one hand and the opposite leg were pressed securely against earth. Her weight shifted, so if her next step did not find purchase, she would not fall into a bottomless chasm.

Let me out..., the voice emerged again. Echo silenced it temporarily. It was persistent and alien, he considered distancing himself from his rider. Having her embrace him only put her in proximity with an unknown force. "Helena, my back is tender. Can you sit more upright?"

Get this skin off with her...

"Lord Echo, I would like to walk, actually. For a moment. Might be best for your back and for my legs."

He stopped. Bryhan helped her dismount.

"You will slow us," Grave said. Receiving glares from Echo and Bran he added, "But we must balance helping everyone recover with making haste."

Being blindfolded and carried she had been disoriented, but on her feet, touching the walls and smelling the air, Helen knew immediately their specific location. Her living quarters were up two levels from here, including a short trip over a limestone bridge toward the west. Walls once hewn smooth became ragged here; farther along, it would become less carved but still flat. Eventually the corridor was irregularly skewed. Frequent jutting formations protruded from the wall, signaling a transition to lower strata.

The smells of the musty corridors were familiar too. Helen had always steered clear of the network of gibbets within the Doctor's dungeon. There, the scents turned most foul: excrement, salty sweat, and acrid bile. She smelled some of these now. Bryhan hastily grabbed her to ensure she did not fall off the edge of an encroaching precipice. The walls had opened up abruptly. Burden and Ruhyn gasped looking at the canyonesque dungeon before them.

"What is it? What do you see?" Helen asked.

Ruhyn awed, "We're seein' depths and heights beyond measure, and they're going down as far as the mountains of Tonn are high. Cracks 'n crevices 'n chasms branch from each other in all directions. Dotted wit' countless lights, no less. 'Tis like the night sky, 'cept the lights are yellow flames rather than blue stars. Firebrands 'r scurryin' everwhere! I'm guessing those are your fellow Keepers runnin' about, far away. And the monstrous pris'ners. Helen, they're hangin' from endless chains to a roof we cannot see and over chasms withou' any bottoms." Ruhyn and Burden cast a disconcerting look toward the Doctor who maintained the dungeon.

Helen envisioned an imaginary, ensnared hybrid. Contorted within an iron cage too short to accommodate its height, it swayed while screeching weakly, having nearly resigned to its fate. On its belly was the mark of the enemy: a circle radiating six rays. Recalling the attack, she asked anxiously, "Are there chromanti?"

Creatures of all types dangled in nets and nooses, many skewered by rods, Ruhyn observed by lamp light. "I see mutated demons. And winged monsters…all dead or dormant."

"Those are the blue-bloods," Bryhan corrected.

Grave expounded, "Curator, the chromanti hauled in through South Gate cannot be seen from this vantage. We will go near them soon enough."

Bryhan saw her anxiety. She was looking forward to not

seeing them, or even being near them. Echo's thoughts were likewise preoccupied with escaping the presence of the hybrids.

"Follow me." The Doctor led them. "Be aware, we will descend stairs for some time."

Grave gave orders to the Keepers along the way. Some left only to return later in the journey to deliver food rations and flasks of water. Many were instructed to extinguish the torches as they sought hiding places. The great dungeon seemed to collapse under a crushing dimness. The deeper they descended, the darker their passage became.

The gongs' sounding had become muffled. They had ventured far from the populated strata of the Keep. They continued to walk briskly. It was not long until the sulphuric scents of the warning torches diminished. Helen observed the change first, noting that a malodorous damp wafted by her.

"I smell them," Helen said.

Grave confirmed, "The chromanti are incarcerated close to here."

Ruhyn moved his lantern about which failed to illuminate more than a few feet about him.

Burden sniffed. "Devils."

They bypassed bridges that extended into, and over, dark-filled caverns, and through colonnades demarcating the threshold to the lower dungeon. The pathway became grittier. The less traction she sensed, the more she knew they were venturing onto remote pathways. She could not have guessed that Doctor Grave intended to lead them under the Keep, into depths she did not know existed. The puddles she stepped in felt strangely viscous. Each step released the putrescent scent of tar, tinged with sulfur. She recognized the black essence about her. This liquid was connected to the bogs above. The oil seeped under the Land. Its emptiness pulled on her. She longed to be in the upper levels. Even the comfort of ruined Tonn. "Doctor. I loathe this muck."

"Take comfort in that it will likewise affect our enemies. It will shield you from any spells they cast. This oil, the stuff of the bogs, serves as a protective moat."

Helen's disgust was not swayed. Perhaps if she had been a necromancer, then she could have appreciated the oil's alchemical potential. The melancholic liquid had been seeping from the walls and encroaching every trail until they had no choice now but to walk through it.

Helen complained, "I keep stepping in the…ugh. I am taking my bandage off to see—"

"Stop," the Doctor intervened. "Your wound is still healing. You must keep that wrap on until I order otherwise. Your apprehension is not warranted. The oil is rather inert, provided flames are absent. There is no way to keep from getting wet. When we begin to wade in it, we will dowse all the lanterns, save mine."

Wade in it? Helen stumbled along. Bryhan seemed to appear every time she needed a shoulder or hand. When the guard was preoccupied, Ruhyn would assist her. Echo seemed out of reach.

Iron stalagmites lanced up from the black oil. The metal needles were products of alchemy and sorcery. Burden was accustomed to pulverizing ore to feed the smelting furnaces to release the hidden metal; but here, below the Keep, iron grew as colossal crystals from the black oil. These fascinated Burden. He carried his pick and hammer across his back; these tugged on his injured shoulder, and he increasingly found his weapons catching hidden rocks and skeletons. Despite his fatigue, he plodded along.

Helen continued to stagger. Dizzy and tired, she asked, "How long must I remain blind folded?" She waited for the Doctor to answer, but received no answer. Then she slipped abruptly.

Ruhyn caught her by the shoulders. Her pelt, caked with mud, pressed against his mask. "Are you alright?"

Helen returned slowly, "I think I am." She straightened, leaning into Ruhyn for support. "How did I get here? In a remote hole, under the Keep. Serving a Gray. Blind-folded."

"Well, it makes sense that you came to the Keep early on. Qual fell fast in the Ill Age. By the time our Clanlord Kaiyn gathered his Legion, your Qualenson had disappeared. Your clan was in ruin. Where else were you to live?"

Helen began wading through the muck on her own accord. "My home was indeed near Qual, but my family lived on the outskirts. Even the Qual folk from the Keep never seem to recognize my origin. How did you know?"

"I hadn't the years of learnin' you had here, but I know the skin of a mountain cat when I see one. Given the age, size, and condition of that pelt, I'd gamble that came from whence you grew up. Cats like that live 'n the highlands near Qual."

Helen was stunned he knew more about her than any of those from the Keep. He continued, "…as it was, Clan Tonn handled the sorcery better. For a time anyway. Still lost all our mothers to the wills and whims of the demons 'n such. Bryhan's father was a strong Clanlord, led the Legion of Fathers against the devils. Yet he never came back. We may have lost our lords, but we orphans were not leavin' our land without a fight."

Helen interrupted, "But now you find yourself in the Keep?"

"Yes. The last battle forced us here. Burden and I need protection for a time, but we won't stay here. For now, being near our Clanlord is comfortin'. We don't understand sorcery, though we hope he can come back to us. Bryhan denies this is possible. The Gray Lords appear honorable 'nough. But the war they fought, and still fight, is full of dark deeds. Lord Lysis and Doctor Grave strike fear into us. We of Tonn remember their darker selves. They seemed to destroy the Land as much as they protect it."

Finally, the Doctor called for a halt. "We have reached the moat of melancholic oil surrounding the Hollow. We will need mounts to cross it. The soldier ants are all above, so we will call upon the larvalwyrmen. The oil banks soaked Grave's ankles as he moved forward. "Our destination is there," the Doctor pointed upward into the darkness. "You cannot see it now, of course, since lamplight is not bright enough. Know that a giant stalagmite protrudes out of this oily sea. We will ascend it. A twin stalactite extends from above, and at their meeting point lies a hollow chamber. The once-Queen's vault."

Helen tilted her head instinctively upward, tracking the echoes of their conversation. "How high is this cavern?"

"As high as the dungeon chasms are deep," Grave answered with pride, remembering the days when the once-Queen's colony was healthy and her brood carved the first tunnels. "Within, you will be shielded by layers of stone above, air and darkness around, and a sea of larvalwyrmen-infested oil below. There is no other place as remote or protected as this in the Keep. In fact, to enter this secreted hollow we will require the aide of larvalwyrmen." Doctor Grave began chanting while performing a slow dance in which he turned and stomped his feet. From the black liquid wyrms emerged answering his call. Slime coated grubs with leathery backs as thick as mature oak trunks, but flexible as the common worm, writhed onto the shore. Swollen white veins decorated their skin. These were once-Queen's larvae, meeting death before maturing. Possessed with Lord Lysis' *lapis elixir*, they transcended the Ill Age.

"Snuff out your lamps, and follow mine when we go," commanded Grave. They did so out of trepidation, allowing cold darkness to creep over them. "We will ride these worms," Grave explained. "Helen, you must ride again. Lord, can you take her?"

Distracted, Echo did not reply. His antenna trembled intensely. *Let her on you and I will consume her,* warned the alien voice inside him. Only he heard it. *I will devour her…*

"*Lord Echo?*" Bryhan spoke through telepathy. "*It is time to carry Helen again. Are you able?*"

Echo returned to reality, quenching the voice as he

concentrated. *"Yes, Bran."* Then he kneeled beside his curer, "Come here, Helena." Straddling her Lord, they entered the Underworld sea. Helen flinched as the cool, melancholic liquid rose above her feet and climbed her waist.

"Lord Echo, you may commence climbing. I will meet you above," Grave instructed, "Now, Guard Bryhan, climb on top this larvalwyrmen. Assist Master Ruhyn. You two will have to aid the ram-helmed man." The Doctor secured the humans to the larvalwyrmen with several lengths of cords. Then he mounted his own wyrm. "Guard Bryhan will steer. You two must see to holding the lanterns and canteens. For now, your larvalwyrmen will follow me. All you have to do is hang on." Grave and his wyrm glided into the black sea. The humans' eldritch larva followed the Doctor's guide light. "Once I deliver you to the vault, I must head back to the Theater."

Grave's lantern advanced as if levitating on a wave of shadow. Ahead, Echo and Helen trekked out of sight. The calmer Ruhyn supported his friend, who continually shifted position.

"Burden," Bryhan engaged to allay his fears, "Do you not trust my steed?"

Burden scoffed. "Serpents. Evil."

"Captain, the wyverns that plague Tonn are not the same as this. This worm derives from the once-Queen's larvae. The Doctor and Grays command them," Bryhan explained. "The snakes haunting your mines are scaled. They come from a different source."

"Aye, Burden, listen to our Clanlord. He knows the difference. Wyvern armor he wears, after all. We can always trust in Bryhan."

"Doctor. Corrupt."

Guard Bryhan looked over his shoulder at the others, "The Doctor will not harm you."

Stubborn Burden sighed.

"Clanlord, we know that Lysis controls that butcher. Yet his past sticks to 'im. We can't forget the past." Ruhyn explained. "His intentions aren't clear to us. We follow you because the chromanti motives are very clear. They invaded Tonn. Wish we could've handled 'em on our own. Had our city not been 'nihlated I wouldn't be here. This Keep is not welcomin' to us. Burden has reasons not to trust the Doctor."

Bryhan understood, having been maimed by the Doctor himself. As one undead, he since learned that the golem was merely serving a greater cause. "Whatever your fears, you are welcome to stay after this battle," Bryhan countered. "Lysis and Echo are forthright and rule the Keep rationally. The Gray's magical nature, as mysterious as it may be, is exposed for any to study," he paused. "Learning from the Ill Age may be difficult if you relish the past which it destroyed." He considered, *I will never be your Clanlord.* "Parts of the past are truly gone, Master Ruhyn. You may find more joy if you let it fade away."

They passed stone harpies locked in eternal combat with insectan elders. So detailed and abundant were the forms, it was not clear to the Outsiders whether or not they had been carved by hand or born from sorcery. Burden touched one of the sculptures to learn more. "Limestone?" The rock was known to be soft and easily carved, but the origin of all these grotesque sculptures was a mystery to him. What muse would inspire such horrific craft?

"Clanlord Bryhan, this place must have a terrible past." Ruhyn spoke, "All the petrified creatures and men here. Fightin' statues. Half drownin' all around us. What happened here?"

"They are victims of dyscrasia. Hybrid blood always calcifies," Guard Bryhan said. "So goes the Rule of Stone."

"Rules?" Ruhyn sighed, not knowing of Doctor Grave's teachings. "Clanlord, it seems we're seekin' refuge in an ancient battleground. We are surrounded by stone insects 'n winged beasts. A frozen hell, this is."

Bryhan explained, "The Chromlechon Keep has a deep history. Lots of corrupted blood spilled here at the end of the Ill Age. I chased after Echo then, trying to rescue him."

"Clanlord Bryhan, the disease doesn't seem controlled yet by the Grays. Above, hybrids plague the Land to this day."

"The Ill Age is over," continued the undead Guard. "The Grays contain the disease. The chromanti are a new threat. They also do not originate from the Chromlechon. They came from an unknown origin, arriving through Tonn's mines."

"Well I would agree they came through the mines, but not from them. I fathom they came from beyond or below. That mystery is of no matter now, since they have overrun the City. My captains fell 'neath the spires and fallen forges. Far as we know, Burden and I are the only survivors."

"I am certain more survive," Bryhan said, "though they are surely scattered. Are you still motivated to restore Tonn? If not, the Keep would welcome you."

"I intend to restore the City. I love nature's wealth inside the Land, but people 'r meant to live free of walls. I still need you, Clanlord Bryhan. Although you serve Echo now, I hope you can lead our clan…your clan…again someday." He took a moment to cherish a memory of Tonn's grandeur, enriched in his imagination.

"That is your charge now, not mine, Master Ruhyn. Must I remind you again that I am dead, sir? I cannot be the Clanlord you wish me to be. The royal family you wish to lead you is no longer."

"How long must you serve Echo?"

"Until he decides to release me, or when he dies. Either way, I will return to a true, still death. Hold fast to a new future, not ghosts of the past. You do not need me to return Tonn to greatness. Its future is in your hands." Guard Bryhan paused. "Hold on now, we ascend."

Grave maintained his lamp, but he was further up and the light did little to illuminate the stalagnate pillar for those who trailed.

Black liquid lapped at their sides as the serpentine creature exited the black sea. The wyrm they rode began its vertical climb bathed in darkness. It contorted about itself, wrapping its crew as would a python, though without harmful intent. Both humans leaned forward to counter the pull of gravity, gasping as air squeezed from their lungs. Up it took them, assuming a contorted knot at its midsection to ensure its passengers did not fall into the abyss. It coursed over a protruding horizontal overhang, which it did with speed. It crawled upside down for a time, before righting itself and continuing its vertical ascent. Finally the wyrm entered a twisted tunnel and deposited them into the Hollow. A modest light lit the vault, the glare of which could not transmit through the tortuous path out.

Before they could recover their breath, Grave turned to leave. "Having delivered you, I must ascend and tend to the Keep's surface, and even grab a prisoner for Lysis en route. If this event turns to an extended siege, expect me to return."

H ELEN DISMOUNTED AND collapsed on weak legs. Bryhan, Echo, and Ruhyn checked on her immediately. They led her away from the entry, deposited her on a rock bed, and crowded around. The rush of attention was overwhelming.

"I am fine," she pushed them away, shaking. She checked her inventory: her paint bladders seemed to be in good condition; even her pelt. "I misplaced my flag."

Bryhan said, "No you haven't. The Doctor used it to wrap your scalp."

"You're now masked like we Outsiders."

"Oh, Ruhyn, I will attend to Burden once I check on my master. Foundling Echo, where are you?"

Echo glided within reach. She could not see his shakiness, but his voice was unsteady. "Helena, I am here. You fared worse than I did, though I still require your skills. First, you should know more about your own injury."

"I am excited to see again. I am already tired of being

blindfolded."

Bryhan placed the cloth bag into Helen's hands. She asked, "What is it? It is tied shut."

"Your right eye is injured, but may heal. Time will tell. And your left eye," Echo paused, "is in that pouch."

She did not expect that. Had everyone not been so silent, she may have thought they were jesting. Helen's mind filled with disquiet. Suddenly, her eye socket felt emptier. It ached to tear, but could not. She groped the air with one hand and found someone else's. It was warm: Ruhyn's hand. Her trembling shook him. "What do you expect me to do with this? Just take it away," she shuddered.

Ruhyn interrupted, "I will take it for now, if you want. When peace reigns ag'in, I will restore 'r forges and make you the finest glass eye ever crafted. My father had blown dozens of eyes for Clan Qual's dolls. Taught me well, he did. Look real as ever. First thing I will make will be an eye for you."

Helen shoved the pouch at him. Her mind replayed memories of Sharon holding the intricate doll from Clan Qual. She imagined a doll with one eye.

"Helena, do not despair. Look past the injury. What defines you is much more than your sight. We need your skills urgently." Echo kneeled, for his legs were weak from travel and battle. Then he spoke faintly, "It pains me deeply to see you harmed."

She felt around her head and felt for relics beneath the bandage. Echo saw her aura calmed as she located her collection of charms. The shade of the mountain cat swatted away the manifestations of fear, and settled into lounging on her neck. She let her fingers move automatically.

"You deserve more time, but ...I...need...," Echo began to lean awkwardly. He collapsed toward her.

"Lord!" Bryhan caught his master's seizing body. Collecting his master aside. "Helen, we need you now."

Someone placed her paints and belongings in her lap. Her thoughts became a muddle of anxiety, fear, and hope. By necessity or desperation, she began to think on her duty: she was tasked to care for her Lord, and had to rely on touch for the time being. Her selfish emotions were stored away, her training taking charge.

Bryhan seated his master on a rock beside his curer. Echo's head swam unsteadily as Helen began to work. The Gray watched her, slowly regaining coherence. Astral hybrids spawned from his shell and moved onto her. These were quickly attacked by her cat spirit, which, having its sleep disturbed, extended its watch to include Echo's body. It crawled down her bandaged head, assuming an emerald hue as it brushed past Sharon's ribbon. As the wispy demons emerged, the cat spirit ate them diligently.

Her inking lost its hue, stoking his aura. She drew beautiful images of dark subjects. They were still emotive and energizing, but concerning: patterns of stars and a six-rayed sun. As Helen purged her mind, she was unaware that she marked her Lord with sacred glyphs of the hybrids.

"Lord, she is marking you like the enemy," Bryhan cautioned.

"Bran, she is only acting as a medium." Echo knew that her inking served to heal herself as she rejuvenated his *lapis elixir.* Still, he felt uneasy with the symbols being placed on him. He consumed these tattoos with haste.

Helen began drawing one-eyed dolls, miniature cyclopses akin to the ragdoll that Sharon once had. Then she drew animal faces, feline helmets, iconic mud masks of those she saw die. Straight bars, angled and crossed, representing her warrior friends. "Lord, tell me what happened to you. Does hybrid blood infect your skin?"

"Ichor was sprayed everywhere, Helena. Six of them pulled my legs and arms apart. Unlike the humans that were splayed this way, they did not tear me asunder. It was then that I read their souls for what motivates them."

"What did they want?"

"They share a common vision of their hybrid Empress. They serve her fervently. They held me aloft by pulling each of my limbs. But they did not do more than superficially cut me and bruise me."

"Ruhyn's companions were not spared?"

"Burden and Ruhyn managed to escape with us." Echo said. Helen tried not to imagine the quartering of Ruhyn's captains and the mud-masked boys. Hidden under the Keep, they waited for the hybrid army to attack, but Echo knew that they had already breached the Keep, in substance, if not form. Alien phantoms appeared, pallid ghosts scintillating before him, anchored to his flesh and shell. He had been marked for sure. His eyes were drawn toward the floating beauty. The Empress was mysteriously attractive: slender cheekbones, two large eyes and three ocelli between. Tendrils of her poisonous ether stretched outward. Spreading to Helen. Echo jerked away from the haunting face, moving away from Helen.

"My apologies, Lord. Did I hurt you?"

The vision of the succubus dissipated. "No. I was startled."

"Where are you? I thought I felt a strange bump." Helen moved toward his voice. Finding him, her hands searched his body. Her fingers ran across an anomalous swollen texture under Echo's foreleg. It was no bigger than an insect bite. "Lord, I did find a wound on your shell. A puncture perhaps."

"Where?" Haunting memories of the chromanti flashed through his mind. Echo felt the pain of being stretched again, pangs of transient cramps, and the coolness of being wetted by their spray. Had he been stung? If so, he had not known. "Are there others?"

Helen searched his limbs thoroughly. "Yes. Two others on your left legs. They are subtle. But the chitin is softer there."

Echo thought to himself, *A new shell grows beneath anyway. If it is contaminated, then it is beyond repair.* He contorted his body to examine the spots. *Her minions must have stung me. Helena's arts were needed to find these wounds, but they cannot cleanse my blood.* He saw wisps of white ether leak from the wounds. *My soul is corrupted, Helena. You cannot remove what is now inside me.* "My body is fine now," Echo used his hands to brush the persistent, haunting women's face from his mind. "Thank you, Helena."

Echo angled Helen over to Burden. "Fire clean," he explained as she examined his wound. Repeated cauterizations had confounded the deep laceration on his shoulder: the application of fire had stopped the bleeding, yet abscesses swelled and required draining. She emptied these. Had she sight and the proper threads, she would have attempted to sew portions of the wound together. Instead, Burden handed her a smoldering stick which she used to selectively treat tangential wounds. With one hand she located targets, and the other she applied heat. Each use extinguished the flame, and the unflinching Burden would reignite it for her. She had Ruhyn hydrate her rabbit-skin powder with thyme, which she applied as a poultice.

With Burden cared for, she could rest. The smell of smoldering skin had made her dizzy, and the traumatic day had caught up with her. She fell fast asleep, completely exhausted.

GRAVE ENTERED SOUTH Gate courtyard, wheeling a cart. A chromantaur lay sedated within a gibbet on its wooden bed.

Lysis called from the ramparts, "Doctor Grave, come to the wall. The enemy army arrives."

The golem deposited the cart at the base of the ramparts. "One moment, my Lord."

A band of curers circled about the Doctor, ready to assist. They watched him retrieve three circles of cartilage; they did not know that they had been punched from a Grey Lord's shell. Grave finalized his surgery on the unconscious prisoner by sewing them equidistantly into a triangular pattern between the creature's two, great eyes. In moments, the three coins of Echo's sloughed flesh adorned the forehead of the prisoner. Infused with *lapis elixir*, they transmuted into veined opal, or so it appeared to the living. The undead saw burning embers of white fire.

The curators analyzed the broken body with sustained disgust. Not only was it repulsive as a creature, its white blood was a novel threat to be feared. Worse now, Doctor Grave had altered it. No longer did it appear feminine, as it had when Lord Lysis had captured it. Its chest had been smoothed, its head sculpted.

"Repair its scars. Spread the aura of its new eyes across its head." Doctor Grave ordered the retinue. The curators brought the cart toward the giant pyre, and tended to their patient both cosmetically and aurorally. He climbed the steps up the crenelated wall.

Grave approached Lysis. "Your decoy is nearly readied."

"And the others?" Lysis maintained his gaze from the Chromlechon Keep.

"I brought them to the Hollow as you desired, my Lord."

Lysis turned. He was not worried about Echo. The Foundling could take care of himself. He was concerned about the children, the parentless youths of the Keep. Most of the maidens became initiates of the Gray. The eldest ones manufactured paper in the mills alongside the outer Keep; they lived there too, in the Grottos, some with their own infants. An army of children had become parents themselves, and they were not prepared to defend themselves. "The Keepers, Doctor. Tell me their status."

Grave clarified, "The Grotto Folk are mostly within the Keep, though some linger outside. The Red Caps are nestled away beyond reach. The young take care of the younger. They are safe and ready for siege."

The two looked outward together. Before them, beyond the embrasure of the Keep's ramparts, they saw the morning sun shine upon the army's back. It had approached overnight under the cover of darkness. The soldiers were not attempting to hide. With unnatural speed, they had come from the eastern mountains. The hybrids organized a camp a mile outside the bogs. Their behavior troubled Lysis, since it violated his assumption that nonhumans were not ordered or civil. The Keep appeared disorganized beside them.

Lysis saw only two types of visitors: humans requiring rescue, and the enemies that held them. The humans were caged. The menagerie of creatures the Grey Lord saw with equal disdain: giant eagles, winged humans with bird legs, giant ants like the once-Queen he rode upon, humans with arthropodal legs like Echo, and humanoids with ant heads.

Doctor Grave saw otherwise. The golem was struck by the common underlying biology amongst the enemy. All expressed some combination of three phenotypes: avian, insectan, human. The golem had names for most. The unmixed species included: rocs, being the gargantuan birds that were as large as the deceased Avian King, whose bones were entombed within the Theater below; the insectan elders, the colossal ants which created him, and for which he once served; and the humans. Then there were the hybrid variations: the sylphin, the horse sized, insectan-avian hybrid that was cousin to the griffin; harpies, the avian-human hybrids with human torsos with bird legs and wings; chromanti, the insectan-human hybrids; and the chepri, the ant-headed humans.

Grave also saw that the simplest types, being the non-hybrids, had red burning souls. The hybrids burned white. "There is more to blood and soul that I must understand," Grave spoke. "The bodies of our visitors are a mystery, some alchemy that we have yet to master."

"And if we understood the nature of their blood, what would we be doing differently that we cannot do now?"

"Why Lord, we could go beyond controlling dyscrasia. We could eradicate it altogether."

Lord Lysis grew agitated, "You deem my hunting insufficient."

"Your solution to kill them all, applied over twenty years, has only increased their numbers." Lysis' anger flared. Grave hastily explained, "Lord, we must learn more about the disease's origins. If we knew how it spawned, then we could derive a lasting solution."

Just a day ago, the forest about the Keep was empty. Then came the ant-headed chepri, holding their banners high, riding their captive sylphin with high esteem. Their mounts had had their wings clipped, so they lumbered along on the land. They were disabled captives, but they were not possessed. The lances were held vertical; black pennants flapped from them, adorned with a white circle crowned with six rays. Incense censers dangled on chains from the spear tips, smoke churning in streams in both astral and corporeal realms. A hundred standards spread out into six regular intervals, as per the sigil.

"Those pennants are magical."

"Lord, the kindling pneuma emitting from them must be energy vessels for their leader."

"So, the bearers are like my curers. You expect a sorcerer."

"These pawns require a commander. I observe none yet. I am reading their thoughts…they await for a Queen … no… an Empress. She must bring a sorcerer with her."

The royal army came next. The warrior train of chromanti had crawled out of the mountains from Clan Tonn, over the trodden Gorgepath of the valley, toward the Keep. The Gorgepath was so congested, the dense swarm of locust–men spilled over its boundaries and infiltrated the forested vale. The cedars and pines could not contain this infestation. The leafy foliage of the Land appeared less and less green, less natural, more smooth and reflective. Soon, the forest seeped as would a saturated sponge. The enemy horde spilled around the bog.

Within a league of the Keep, the influx separated into six clusters, a close-packed hexagonal pattern. Concerted in their undulating advance, the soldiers subdivided within the confines of the grid. Each cluster was organized into many sub-regiments. A large void was maintained at their center, matching that of the node on the six-rayed sun sigil. The spying Keepers imagined this formation as a Compass Rose on the Land. The Northwest and Southwest regiments were closest to the bog; the two eastern complements were farthest away from the Keep; the remaining two marked the true North and South azimuths.

The real sun was present enough, and shone upon their enemies' bone armor as they neared.

"These hybrids dress in the skin of others. Just as my Picti ancestors dressed in eldritch shells." Lysis leaned on the stone wall. "Grave, I do not detect any males."

"Those soldiers below are two-eyed, wingless drones. Fertile males have special sets of eyes and wings to enable nuptial rites. Those are sterile hybrids."

"No fertile males." Lysis concluded.

"That supports our suspicions. All colonies need to re-produce. This one is no different, except it seems to have come a long ways to seek a mate."

"Explain, Doctor. Since Echo does not have the eyes of a fertile male. Why would they seek him so strongly if he were not suitable?"

"He is due to molt presently. His final imago will emerge soon."

Ten thousand strong, the army settled about the pe-rimeter of the Keep. Their forces could not fit on the singular land-bridge crossing the bogs. If only they could be compelled to venture there. They staked camp on the opposite shore within the eerie Grey Orchard, wherein hundreds of creatures were impaled on iron poles, draped across the skeletons of leafless willow trunks, and posed upon crucifixes as if they were spent carcasses. Many were just lifeless skeletons; just as many were infused with Lysis' blood.

"Lord, they do not seem to understand that the Orchard is full of your soldiers."

"Yes, my power within the Gray Horde remains concealed, as is the cavalry of larvalwyrmen beneath the surface of the bogs. The foreigners underestimate us." Lysis' trap was set, but his prey was not all here yet.

The colossal birdcages rolled forth, led by more chepris that held clarions instead of flags. Their avian mounts were rocs, unseen on this Land for centuries. The giant eagles were encumbered with heavy cargo: portable prisons, modified ribcages of their own brethren: gutted, stripped of flesh, and fitted with wheels. The rocs were not designed to haul like beasts of burden. Iron bits silenced their caws. Unfurled, the wings would span more than ten fathoms; mutilated as they were, they would never lift again. Ethereal purple chains wrapped their red shades. They were as enslaved as those within their cages: insectan elders, living ants as large as the once-Queen. Nearly a dozen fit per wagon. Their souls burned as fresh red muses, untapped vessels of profound creativity.

"The elders live, after all," Lysis said.

Awestruck, Grave assessed them. "Those that survive are threatened."

Lysis examined the Doctor's spirit, which reeled from long repressed memories struggling to resurface. Past obligations of nursing eldritch nymphs flashed past. Then the Doctor's own attempts to create life shimmered: astral wreaths of golem babes, and a girl named Maeve.

"Do I need to affirm your conviction, Grave?"

"Your blood is my life, my Lord. My memories are just that. I was created to serve, and serve I do."

More cages rolled into the camps, drawing the skeletal warrior's attention back to the battlefield. He saw humans, hundreds of captive people, yellow-eyed with fever, with green-tinged skin, and hair, frail like sun-bleached grass. Only a few had strength to reach out from the skeletal bars in desperation. Lysis tallied them: seven and six hundred fathers; thirty-three and four hundred mothers; five score sons, and just as many daughters. All with red souls rooted together, indicating they shared a common ancestor. They worshipped some sort of tree.

"Lord, do you see the caged dryads?"

"I see them. They are not of the Clans. Their auras burn differently than the humans from our Land. Still of red hue, like their blood. But of a different intensity. A purer red."

The Doctor replied, "They are close cousins to humans. I do not know where they came from. I predict they are merely fodder for sorcery. Or so I considered such when I served the once-Queen."

"The hybrids keep their ingredients separated: avian; insectan; human. They fear mixing them."

"Perhaps, my Lord, they want to keep their captives alive. If put in the same cage, one would eat the other. Also, these white-blooded hybrids are repulsed by the individual species that comprise them. Lord, clearly you see the segregation of color. The hybrids shy away from their captives as if they are contagious."

Lysis distilled Grave's hypothesis: "They believe the red-bloods are diseased."

Doctor Grave studied the army below. "A healthy hybrid may think that way. Certainly, the enemy treats elders and humans as lesser beings. In any event, they humiliate their conquests. They want us to know that they have conquered before."

"This is more organized than my Queen's colony was," Grave replied. "She and the human Picti were symbiotic, before dyscrasia escalated. All the mutants that survived the Ill Age have been lone predators. Yet this enemy is socialized."

"They are a developed colony, powerful enough to enslave other cultures."

"Lord, they have a common mission and command. There is much we do not know about the opponent at our doorstep." Doctor Grave considered how a population so large could remain hidden. "It would be interesting to follow their trail to discover their origin."

Lysis brandished *Ferrus Eviscamir*. "Yes. Rooting their source is imperative. I will not rest until they are eradicated, and their human slaves freed."

Grave readied his ax. "As it stands now, it is we who are threatened."

"We only need to kill the Empress." Lysis surveyed the Land for their commander amongst the shimmering landscape.

Grave advised, "You must not overlook the army she controls. Her military speaks to her constitution. They reflect her ability. Her strengths."

"I only need her to show herself."

Suddenly, the six wedge-shaped regiments aligned themselves. Six facets, a thousand units each. All facing center toward a vacant space. The hybrid standard-bearers raised their clarions and released their fanfare.

Wwwuuuurrrr! Wurrrrr!

The flag bearers waved their staffs, sounded their horns. To the center, six chromanti crawled forth and emptied bags of ebony dolls: smooth simulacra that were little curled-up, androgynous humans, ants, and birds.

Grave was delighted to see long lost eldritch power in the form of golem hearts. "Homunculi, Lord. We are about to witness an art not practiced here since before I was created by the once-Queen."

Each regiment below ushered forth a roc, harnessed to a bone cage. Three filled with exhausted humans, three with scrambling insects. Ingredients were collected about the pile of black, statuesque homunculi: twenty-one and four hundred fathers; half as many mothers.

Chromantaur spearman nudged them all into a tight circle. They lanced the throats of the rocs, red blood flowed onto the ground. As it became clear they intended to kill their human captives too, Lysis turned with his sword ready. Grave held his arm. "Lord, their fate is already sealed. The army calls their Empress with their sacrifice. We must let them die for her to arrive."

They watched as the hybrids poked and prodded, their bladed poles penetrating the skeletal bars, opening the flesh of their offerings. Lysis' spirit boiled with anger.

The golem delayed the Lord, "Not yet. Attacking before she arrives may prevent her arrival. We must let them finish."

Thus three types of red blood mixed. Liquid veins of blue formed, only to swirl under some arcane force. The mass of bone, blood, and body melted. Blisters on the Land's surface beneath it burst, spewing white spittle. From afar, the Keepers saw the soil under this sacrifice glowing violet, a grand ring of bruised tissue. The earth transmuted to a fleshy translucence. The amalgam at its center reduced itself to a homogenous cream, ribbons of red fading to yellow, fading to white. Roiling within the casein pool was the ebony homunculi: black specks, riding the eddies of necromantic currents.

Lysis identified the liquid, *"Lapis elixir."*

"Aye, Lord. They reverse the nature of our Land's earth, turning it to flesh. They do more than conjure up creatures. They are making a gateway."

A glistening skin formed over the puss pond. Under it, the morass melted stone, and released as a growing pressure swelled the concoction. The globular blister pushed all away from the center. Grass, roots, weeds, all swelled away from the inflating tissue. Errant, uprooted plants appeared like tufts of hair. A conical white pustule remained an earthen bubo.

Wwwuuuurrrr! Wurrrrr!

The sounding of clarions lead a chorus of scratching legs, the insectan appendages of the army forming an orchestra. The strange harmony rippled the crust on the white blister. The coating dilated to reveal a soft, clear globe of turbid jelly. Then it parted like one colossal eye opening.

Wingless, white serpents emerged, reaching toward the Sky like glistening fingers. Wyverns, as wide as a man, with stumpy, frog-like legs, slithering their way out of the gel. Straining themselves upright. Searching for support, they folded onto the ground. The serpents, and the flesh-mud they had traveled through, rolled down the mound, a lather of sienna froth.

A cavity yawned in their wake. An artery penetrating the Land terminated here. The pliant earth heaved, ushering something to the surface. Mucus spewed in pulsing gushes. From the orifice, a cylindrical fusion of flesh and bone crawled from the pit's depths toward the fore. Arms, antennae, talons, and monstrous limbs sprouted from its central backbone, the ground melting under each palm. Countless hands emerged with as many antennae, feeling and probing like wild, sentient hairs. An interlocked mass of meat, with clots of white blood congealing in its folds, writhing like a snake, sliding on a liquid trail. It was not a smooth wyrm. It had no proper head, though several rib bones of the griffins now extended like elephantine tusks from its anterior.

Grave exclaimed, "A behemal centimani! It takes powerful sorcery to raise such a monstrosity, let alone control it. That is not possessed by blood. Rather it has been born from the geomancy, the sorcery that spawned my golem kind. That is a many-bodied, many-hearted assembly."

The behemoth millipede slithered closer now. As it neared, what had appeared to be pale limbs were actually parasitic, white-scaled wyverns. Their heads were anchored to the columnar mass, feeding on red blood. As their tails swayed, they glistened like jewelry. It reached the camp center and stopped. A mass of aligned limbs blossomed open above its tusks. They stood erect in a semicircular frill, exposing a brilliant self-luminous body. Melted earth, veins of red and white, slushed off her. Like a pearl exposed from its clam shell, her body proved glossy and luminous. She was radiant white with a sheen that rivaled the moon's brilliance. Thus the hybrid sorceress revealed herself atop the giant wyrm she controlled. She sat in her grotesque throne of wine-red sinew.

"The Empress!" The Doctor leaned forward in awe.

Angelic, transparent wings had wrapped her. They expanded slowly, unveiling her beauty. As they exposed her torso, they relaxed atop her lower abdomen. Its pearlescent chitin shell shimmered like a polished gem, the sun's morning rays reflecting and making her glow. Ethereally she glowed too, her aura veiling her casein flesh and splendid chest, obscuring her set of elfin breasts with a scintillating fog. More clearly visible were her slender arms, narrow antennae, elongated ears, and her bald head.

Her glowing eyes swallowed everyone's gaze. Between her two primary orbs, a set of three smaller lenses marked the apexes of a triangle. To the naïve, these ocelli appeared as inset jewels. To those who saw as the undead *saw,* they were sources of groping, energetic veins that reached out like snapping whips, connecting fiery ties from her to her standard-bearers. With her at the center, and with rays connecting her radially to her colony about her, her aura mirrored that of her sigil: a sun in the form of a ring, with six rays.

"The Empress is a sorceress, Lord!"

"Then I have but one enemy to slay."

The Empress spoke to her minions now, through her network. She learned that her mate was being hidden in the Keep. She decided to begin her real assault. While the two powerful sorcerers atop the Keep were kept distracted, she covertly cast another spell…

Via telepathy, Echo observed what Grave and Lysis saw above. The mass of rock between blurred the vision. As he strained to resolve the scene, the ghost of the Empress's spirit literally emerged from his own glow. Her halo suffused his, fed him with energy, and stole his focus. Her bodiless fingers took form. Caressing his antennae, she whispered, *"You hide with the Spawnen. You belong with us. Come be with your own kind. Come with me when I call…come, Servandum."*

Her words penetrated his mind, her voice so stark it was if she was speaking into his ears. His fellow humans, the Spawnen as she called them, could not hear her.

Smoky legs entwined about his abdomen, and her arms wrapped about his aura, working it into thread-like lengths. Her many eyes crystalized: two large, three inset between.

"You were born for me," she beckoned. Her lithe, ghost fingers caressed his cheek. She traced a triangle sensuously on

his forehead. Three imprints marked his forehead. Three phantom eyes. *"Your fertility is emerging."*

Bryhan observed his Lord's odd behavior. The Empress's presence escaped the Guard's senses. He mindspoke to Echo, *"Are you well?"*

Echo replied aloud, trying to break himself free from the spell, "I feel the urge to retreat, Bran. Sadly, I have nowhere to go." The Foundling brooded. The alien markings of the Empress still seeped from him. Worse, she could see through his body. Indeed, she was spying on the Keep through him. His skin burned where her invisible hands touched his antenna. Where her legs had wrapped him, he itched.

"Lord, we could induce your molt. Perhaps, reinitiating the rite would make you better."

Echo floundered for an answer. "I must remain strong and delay molting. I fear such an attempt would only weaken me. We must wait until this battle ends. It is best if we finish at the site where I have always transmuted. Not here. Not when the enemy is coming, and Helena is vulnerable. She cannot help easily with her injury. I could not bear to see her die as I saw Sharon, an immobilized, passive witness. Please, tend to the others. I am well enough for now. The others grow curious."

Bryhan obeyed. Echo could feel the Empress's spirit peer over his shoulder as Guard Bryhan left to check on the humans.

Ruhyn hailed, "Clanlord, we found something strange. Little, dried up people. A whole pile of them."

Searching blindly in the rubble, Helen grabbed one.

"Dolls?" She felt the faces of the armatures that were no more than a foot long, but could not find any true eyes or mouth. "Someone describe to me what they look like?"

Smoking sage suddenly overwhelmed her. Burden was smudging whatever she held. "Babies." The ram-helmed man muttered.

"Not people." Bryhan identified them. "Homunculi seeds, more commonly known as golem hearts."

Helen remembered viewing Doctor Grave's exposed heart as he demonstrated the Rule of Blood and Ether. The *lapis elixir* of Lord Lysis leaked from it. *Possess the blood another to control its body. Control its heart to direct its mind.*

Bryhan explained, "The once-Queen animated the golems with the material from within those hulls. With fresh seeds, one can give life to clay. That art of imparting life into earth is all but lost. Our sorcery has evolved toward using blood to animate flesh instead."

"Why would she do such a thing?" Ruhyn asked.

"The once-Queen started her colony alone, or so Doctor Grave told me. She needed help nursing her eggs and pupae, and had a supply of homunculi. So she created her golem helpers in this studio."

The Empress watched upon these relics, and mesmerized Echo into looking too, *"When you come with me, you will see the cruel orchard that bears the fleshy fruit. The homunculi are born on bloody trees, the Ill Orchard, which is the source of the dyscrasia that haunts your Land, creates the Spawnen. You are healthy. You are meant to be with me ..."*

The Empress contorted his soul, formed a virtual brood from his own aura. Echo was also the only one to *see* the hundreds of miniature offspring, astral simulacra, spring from him toward Helen. Echo took a step away and turned. They failed to reach her before dissipating. To shield his eyes from his observations, he stared down into a dark crevice. Therein, the ghost swam in shadow. Waiting for him. Rhythmically swaying beneath him, she parted her lips. He felt their wet contact. Echo recoiled. Multiple, lengthy flames wrapped about him, holding him, but the others could only see his actions…not the spell…

Bryhan asked his Lord, "What is wrong?"

"A mystery troubles me. Hybrids. Humans. Insects and giant birds. The source of dyscrasia and the sharing of energy. Is there is a commonality among us? A common source?"

Helen interjected, "Lord, you speak cryptically. You do not sound well. I will come to you." She stood.

"Stay," Echo spoke more urgently than he intended. *"Bran, I am ensorcelled! What do you see before me?"*

"I see nothing unusual. Are you haunted by something?"

Echo stared at his own spirit. The Empress embraced him still. *"Do you not see it? Them? Her?"*

"Lord, I see only white ether. But no threatening shapes within it."

Of a sudden, the Empress's visage shattered into countless miniature mantises. They crawled over him, knotting wisps of his soul with hers, wrapping him in thin chains. Echo breathed deep. He could control this curse, perhaps. Desperately, he delaminated a bit of skin from his shoulder. He threw it, and the

Empress's white face left him momentarily.

Ruhyn gasped, confused.

Burden rushed immediately to smoke the skin.

Helen grew anxious, "Lord?" She walked apprehensively toward her master, not afraid of him but of boulders impeding her path.

"Bran, you must help cut them off me."

"Master, I still do not know what enemy you see. You mean to flay yourself?" Bryhan restrained his master's arms. *"You must let Helen heal you, provide you with Gray power."*

At first Echo consented. Then he halted. *"Nay, I cannot go near her. They are jumping from me to her. They will poison her too."*

"Jumping? I cannot see them. Where are they?"

His curer got close. Fiery insects bounded onto Helen. Three crawled atop her head. They disappeared into straggly white hair. Her ethereal cat pounced! It swatted, and Helen groped, as if she too were a cat clawing the air. She knew not that her master was the source. Confused, she twirled, and then swooned.

"She has fainted!" Ruhyn collected her, and lay her aside.

Echo stumbled away. His Guard followed.

"Bran, get them off us!"

"I cannot see what you see, master."

Echo spoke to Bryhan, *"You must keep me...away from Helena...the others. At least until I know I will not hurt her."*

"Lord, I think you need to molt. We never finished your

molting ritual, Lord."

Echo reluctantly nodded in agreement. He privately feared that molting may only transform his body as the Empress desired. Into a mature mate. Was there no safe path forward? Was there no way to control one's purpose? After searching for purpose for so long, what if an undesired one came to claim him? Could he successfully deny that?

"Just keep me away from the others. I need space. Time."

"Helen? Perhaps she can help?"

"Helena cannot do more than she has already, Bran. I have been corrupted by a sorceress, a ghostly Empress that works with lapis elixir. Her arts cannot help. Look what I have done to her!"

"I will get you to the Doctor's theater."

"Nay, Bran. Grave could not see my infliction earlier. He cannot remove what he cannot see."

"What then, Lord?" Echo walked past his guardian. Bryhan grabbed Echo and brought his arms down. *"Lord, you are entranced."*

Echo jolted back to reality. The succubus split into several transparent visages, all connected to him via the ether, but hiding in his peripheral vision. *"You must....attack her..."*

"Attack whom?" Bryhan struggled surveying the ether. *"There remains nothing on you that I can see."*

"I will have to figure a way to deal with this myself. Stand guard, Guard Bryhan. Keep the others away until I gain control. We must not alarm the humans. Knowing a spirit

threatens us will only terrify them, since they are not empowered to see or defend against it."

Echo retreated voluntarily to hide in a narrow crevice. Aside from the others, he shivered, cradling his own arms. The ghostly succubus assumed a singular body as large as he was. He became lost in her set of hypnotic eyes. Echo observed this other entity obediently. The female hybrid grew on his own sense of self. Did she share his soul? The more he analyzed the more he lost his volition.

His gaze turned to the star tattoo on her chest, a circle with six rays framed between two engorged breasts. The ghost grabbed his hand and laid it on the sun. Echo's heart raced. His right hand levitated, feeling the air. Beguiled, he did not move. Two inviscid hands pressed against his, locking it in place between them in a cold press. The *lapis elixir* within his arm raced. Then she lifted his hand, and placed his fingers into her mouth. Her lips clasped and sucked. White blood surged.

For hours, Echo remained apart. The Outsiders knew not what to do except protect Helen and look toward their Clanlord for guidance. Clanlord Bryhan was in turn watching his master, solemly, his spear *Aleece* ready. The earth rumbled… his scale armor rattled…and his Gray Lord shook like a maniac…

IV: Bog Battle

The Empresses' magical web resonated around her. Pulses of energy sparkled, spiraling along astral pathways from the chepris' flags toward their center, where she remained enthroned atop the behemoth. Her every move was being scrutinized. This she knew.

Lysis observed his opponent now carefully. The Doctor grew anxious for orders. "Will you charge her?"

"She weaves a trap." Lysis withdrew from the ramparts, striding to his Pyre. "Her sorcery is strongest at the center of her army. I will not meet her there. Instead, I will draw her out."

"What are you doing?" The Doctor asked, following behind.

Lysis had stepped into his fire. Sparks cascaded from his legs. Orange flames heated his armor. Satiated from the mystical bath, his aura burned brilliant white. The lord bent over to sift his hands through the ash. He found a papyrus sheet amongst the burnt offerings, folded it, and then tempered the form with an extended arm. "Preparing an invitation."

"You invite the enemy Empress into the Keep?"

The skeletal warrior cupped his hands, blew into them, feeding the flame that was the burning messenger's life force. "Nay. Only to the causeway in the bogs. To deal, face to face."

"Lord, to what end does a discussion lead?"

"Battle is the only end," Lysis growled. "To begin with, I isolate her from her nexus of magic. You will come with me."

"Should I ready my ax? Or shall I bring the decoy?"

"Both."

Grave began to hail the liverymen, and directed the curators to mount.

"No need for them, Doctor. My retinue will stay behind the walls."

"Very well, Lord. And your means to replenish your power if needed?"

The death's head replied. "I have plans. If the need arises."

"So we alone go down?"

"Once she accepts." Lysis released the sprite. It navigated the wind with the indirect grace of a falling snowflake. Turbulence rocked its delicate wings. Drafts along the mountain carried it on tumultuous currents, over the still black bogs, through the gauntlet of the advancing rays, toward the Empress.

From the ragged walls of the Chromlechon Keep, within deep recesses hidden from the sun, the Grotto Folk that were too curious to seek shelter watched. These children remained paralyzed by deafening sounds. No longer did they hear the creaking of their paper mill, rotating beneath the waterfall without supervision. The mill was running itself, and now rogue, untreated sheets took flight from the press. These strained to join the magical invitation's trajectory, which was guided by the magical harmonics of kerning hybrids toward its proper destination. The Folk watched their Lord's note fly over the tall grass that surrounded the bogs, the very fields used to make paper. Over the naked trees within the tar pits, along the corridor between the first of two clusters of the army it raced, toward the center of the six-pronged star.

The Empress sat upon her golem centimani, her pearly hands taking hold of the sprite. She was not accustomed to the possession of inanimate objects, so the invitation's movement was a curiosity. She released it when its message was theatrically delivered. Leaning forward, her mount began to move her from the center of her mobile colony toward the bogs. Her behemoth was empowered by the homunculi, not her own blood, yet still obeyed her command. The many-bodied thing crawled with wyverns anchored to its sides by their sucking mouths, swaying on it like thick hairs.

"She accepted your message, my Lord."

Lysis moved immediately out of South Gate on the back of the once-Queen. Following, the Doctor descended the mountain trail while pondering Lysis' sovereignty and history. The Chromlechon colony was under attack again. The current Lord went to defend it as a lone fighter. Granted Lysis had his regiment of curators on standby atop the mountain; however, they were not proper warriors. He employed his magical powers to animate an army. His Grey Horde was an extension of himself, as were the ancient larvalwyrmen possessed by his blood. Lysis did not share his duties with his colony.

On the other hand, this Empress led a collective force, her own colony. Each drone lived for her sake. She was a sorceress, powerful enough to reanimate golems. The Doctor mused: What would happen if Lysis was outmatched? If a new queen was here to take over the colony? If the Keep fell to her, then the human orphans would be like those in the enemy camp: fodder for sorcery. If Lysis fell, Grave's heart would fail; however, this sorceress knew enough geomancy to grant the Doctor a new life with a replacement heart. He may serve a third master after all.

The Doctor kept his distance with his covered cargo. Lord Lysis proceeded ahead. The Empress sauntered toward him, her army a furlong behind. The two met on the causeway. It was the sole bridge crossing the bogs, connecting the Keep to the solid Land.

The golem could not discern which was the more monstrous: Lysis or the Empress. Which one was more evil? More righteous? Or were they of the same temperament?

Lysis was a skeletal, human warrior. His dominance was expressed by riding his principal conquest, the once-Queen, whom he slew and then reanimated with his own blood. He was a defender of humans; a slayer of the inhuman.

The Empress he faced was a unique sovereign over a creature colony. She was a living royal hybrid, riding a monster she conjured from alien alchemy. She was indifferent to humans, using them for sorcery or sustenance.

They met. Opposing, celestial auras lashed out to test,

and reject, one another. Again and again their wraithlike filaments clashed, and confirmed that they were of the same white fire. Compatible in composition, yet with repelling force.

The army still sounded its insectile calls until the Empress raised her hand. The Sky and Land seemed to shudder as the atmosphere stilled. Silence settled over all.

The duel began...

ECHO REMAINED DISTANCED from the others, being continuously harassed by invisible swarms. Alone and mostly out of sight, he swatted at his corrupted shade. The Hollow's interior was far from smooth, and the tooth-like formations created circuitous tunnels, crags, and obstructions. Bryhan took position between his lord and the others to block anyone watching.

Meanwhile, Burden was nervously pacing the Hollow. He had mapped the area as best he could. He was experienced in exploring subterranean quarries and knew that passages needed to be traveled from multiple trajectories for one's mind to register the lay of the land. Caverns never looked the same way when backtracking or retreating. A small garden of pyritic crystals caught his attention. The Keep certainly had a wealth of minerals. Yet it was an eerie place, too, with unclean substances like the ominous oil. He compulsively smudged every spot of it on his clothes, and the space around Ruhyn and Helen. Then he extinguished his smoke stick by pressing its embers into his flesh.

Burden watched Echo despite the interrupted view. Echo was striking at shadows. He was convinced Echo needed his aura cleansed with smoke. Bryhan denied him the opportunity. This bewildered the Outsider. Burden did not understand the Grays' power. However, he did trust Master Ruhyn enough to abide his leadership, and since Ruhyn respected Bryhan's conduct so did Burden. He renewed his patrol about the chamber when suddenly a mild earthquake shook the Hollow. Everyone inside prepared for aftershocks, shifting their balance, and bracing their stances as everything vibrated. The shaking chilled everyone's nerves. Something had rattled the Underworld. Was it from the surface?

"Quake," whispered Burden.

No one replied. All knew that what they feared was true. The enemy had reached the Keep. They froze in their battle positions.

Again, the ground trembled ominously. Helen's sleeping body vibrated. The shaking caused her to mumble. Her arms floundered about.

"She is having nightmares," Ruhyn said. "Helen...I cannot wake her."

Bryhan alerted Echo. Called from the shadows, Echo emerged hunched over and sweating. He gathered his resolve. Could he help her safely? What if the Empress affected her now?

Feverishly, Echo went to her.

Ruhyn moved away from Helen's side.

Echo *read* Helena's nightmares: translucent chromanti

sailing on red flames toyed with the sky-colored spirits anchored to her relics. Her soul now searched for her eyes that had escaped her skull in the burning cabin. Her cat spirit lunged trying to catch them. Instead the spirit paws swatted Helen's fears, temporarily keeping them from forming into a stronger substance.

She is not afraid of me... or the curses attached to me, but she reminiscences and is afraid for her homeland, and the wildfires that ravaged her home. She is afraid of losing her sight and being hunted by hybrids, but is not infected by them. The Empresses' poison has yet to stick to her. She is stronger than I thought.

Echo tried to soothe Helen. He had to craft an illusion, but any effigy of himself might carry the Empress's corruption. It would be safer to draw upon a human's shade. He manipulated the ether so that Ruhyn's spirit appeared, riding his own ghostly mountain cat with his fanged helm. The Outsider blew green fire though his pipe. Magical darts took down the wildfire fairies. Then white luminous spheres rolled about, and Helen and Ruhyn's spirit tried to catch them as the fiery demons rolled them away.

Helen awakened startled, panting; this was the first she did so knowing that she was blind. Sudden darkness welcomed her. She reached for something that would help her discern dreams from reality.

"Helena, I am here." Echo placed an antenna into her hand, comforting her slightly.

She described her nightmares. "I dreamt about the day

my home burned. I ventured into the fire to save my parents. They were all gray. Their skin was so scabbed it looked like cracked, dry mud. Heat made my eyes swell, growing bigger and bigger until they came out of my head. They wobbled on the floor like glass marbles, clinking against things without end. As I reached to grab them, my eyes lurched and evaded me. My vision toppled as they rolled. They looked back at my body on occasion. I…it…was completely disoriented. Then Ruhyn appeared and drug me out of the cabin."

I am sorry you have been harmed. Echo sensed Helen was calming to a lesser state of anxiety as she verbalized her fantasy. "I understand. I have nightmares too."

"What scares a Gray Lord?"

Echo glared at the white ghosts emanating from where he had been marked. "Helena, an Empress haunts me with some type of sorcery. Her essence sticks to me like a pall. I cannot look away. I am not certain if I can dispatch her."

"Her mark on your skin ails you? Shall I clean you again?"

You cannot rid yourself of me…

"I fear her mark is permanent, Helena."

She attempted to contain her sadness and gather some resolve. She began casting about for her paints. "I do not know how to stop your nightmares and visions. I have other skills. "

"My mere presence is harming others. That pains me. I would rather free you and Bryhan from the danger that follows me." Echo's antennae lay on her shoulder. "Helena, you are a good soul. I cannot heal your sight without also risking infecting you. I could reanimate your eyes. Though you would see as Bryhan does. And if harm came to me, you would feel it more strongly due to that sorcery. I fear I cannot help you without also subjecting you to more injury."

"I have one eye still. I may be fine. But you still suffer. I must—"

He hushed her response. Wormy ghost fingers extended from his hands. He drew away from her.

"Lord, do not go. I must try something..."

From within himself, Echo's alien personality taunted him: *Go back to her. I want to taste the Spawn's soul. I am hungry to touch flesh...I am coming for you...*

Echo backed away. "You have done what you can." The Gray Lord hailed the leader of the Outsiders. "Ruhyn. come here, please. See to Helen."

I come to get you...

The Foundling left his curator's side to join his guardian. The quaking began again. Helen was left speechless. She held onto Ruhyn's shoulder for support.

The Empress stared at her opponent from atop the centimani; behind her, beyond the black waters, was her army. Her lustrous, inviting eyes were silled with seductive lashes; the three smaller eyes between glistened like diamonds. Her pale human torso skin morphed seamlessly into the pearlescent chitin of her thorax. With her stole of human hair elegantly draped around her arms, she silently assessed the alien warrior.

Yards nearby on the same sodden land-bridge, Lysis presided atop the reanimated once-Queen. The insectan beast he rode on was possessed by his fire, which seemed bizarre to the Empress; her minions may have been drones, but they were alive. Indeed, she had given birth to them. On the other hand, Lysis had an army of raised corpses and possessed manikins. He was not a king as much as he was a singular sorcerer with a horned crown. His earthen servant, a golem, had trailed with a cart that reeked of the Empresses' own phantasmal markings… and…of a maturing male.

The bloodshot eyes of the Keepers, who stared from the distant mountain, stayed captivated, unwilling to blink and miss any moment of this historic encounter: two demigods from different worlds meeting to parley, a brutal humanoid versus an ornamental hybrid. Would another Ill Age begin today for the inhabitants of the Chromlechon Keep? Could the beauteous creature defeat their protector? Enslave them? They could not fathom anything besting Lord Lysis in combat. On the other hand, they had never seen so many creatures threaten the Keep.

The youthful audience may have felt more secure had they been privy to their Lord's plan. They, like the enemy Empress, could not see or sense the wyrms through the black melancholy. The Folk could see the Grey Horde remain still, crucified about the naked tree trunks; the enemy had settled amongst the Lord's skeletons, manikins, and discarded molts, unaware of the Horde's potential. The hybrids were not accustomed to dealing with the raised dead. Possession of inanimate objects was foreign to the chromanti.

The enemy soldiers longed for the covered creature in the cart. They sensed their colony's marking and wanted the prize. If not for their Empress's presence, they would storm the marshes to secure it in her name.

Lysis remained composed. The combined desires of a thousand creatures did not sway him. He was ever confident.

His adversary waved her arms in a graceful manner. Her movements cast ethereal marionettes. One characterized the skeleton dismounting, laying down his sword.

Lysis shook his head. "I do not surrender."

He strained to read her mind. Her shade could not come into focus. If she carried memories and emotions with her, they were veiled. She concealed them, as did he. As his tendrils of white ether probed hers, variegated sparks arced. Puffs of clouds erupted as the blue lightning dissipated. Orange flames emerged, turned gray as they were consumed by sorcerer and sorceress. Their energies waned, waxed, flared white again. Neither succumbed to the other's hypnotic fire.

The Empress likewise surveyed her enemy intently. She showed no alarm, but her centimani investigated the earth compulsively. Its grabby hands fidgeted incessantly, blistering the soil upon contact. As the fleshy behemoth grabbed the stalks of dead grass, they transmuted to bundles of orange human hair. Exposed, curly mangroves, when touched by the behemoth, changed into colorful, knotted entrails and boneless, extended limbs. The fingers of the beast restlessly explored the grotesques it created, tickling the root-flesh into spasms.

Lysis' power compensated immediately, using sorcery to keeping the Land as it was: colored flesh-soil drained immediately, to a dull gray, toward ashen earth.

Elsewhere, opaque stones softened into warm bone with blood-seeping marrow. Stagnant mud congealed into pus-coated sinew. Dead trunks become alive, malleable. The Empress's art gave life back to the dead bogs. This exchange stopped at the water's edge. The centimani probed the oil, but found no purchase. Here, the bog's power stopped the hybrid's sorcery, since its cold, liquid melancholy was inert. It was irreversibly dead; indifferent to her spells.

The Empress stayed resolutely composed, but signs of her spell casting were evident in the distance. Imperceptible streams of energy maintained her strength, continuously consuming her captives. Their depletion went unseen by the Chromlechon champion and his Spawnen hiding in the mountains.

"My Lord, she hides her intentions well. She may be stone faced, but her army reveals her needs transparently. They feel their target is close. They want what is in the cart."

"I can see their intentions, Grave. The cargo you carry is for them. Be ready."

"I know what you came for," Lysis addressed the Empress. "You are in need of a mate. I have what you seek. You know that or you would not be here. We can avoid battle for a fair trade. What would you give for him?" His words were translated theatrically by papyrus minions who orbited around the pair.

She opened her arms. Wind extended the fine hairs of her stole. Her chepri answered, commanding the great eagles forward, dragging bone cages toward the causeway. Inside the bone cages, red-souled insectan beasts clamored.

She spoke an ancient eldritch language. "Your golem servant," the Empress pointed to Grave first, then to the cages, "He wants these."

"Her offering," The Doctor interpreted.

"She reads your desires, Grave, not mine." Lysis shook his head. Indicating the mount beneath him. "I loathe such beasts."

"You harbor Spawnen. You must want mine." Two more rocs clambered forward, several dozen humans inside their cages.

"My Lord, she is disgusted by the humans, elders, and birds. That which we see as purified she sees as a corrupted. Now she reads your soul, my Lord. Your motivations are clear to her."

"I give you both. In exchange for him," she offered.

Lysis nodded in agreement, reading the emotions of his enemies. *"We need not convince her. Just her pawns. They fear losing their prize. I'll mold their fear into realistic visions. They will turn on each other... hybrids will appear as humans and elders. Time to end this ruse."* Raising his left hand high, "Doctor Grave. Roll forth our offering."

A few Grotto Folk still watched with bated breath from the Chromlechon. They saw the wagon roll toward the Lord and Empress. Oppositely, the hybrid army watched intensely. Their anticipation burned as a white conflagration. Their clarions called harmoniously. Their treasure was so close…

Lysis began to lift the canvas, revealing chitin legs. He fueled their excitement, dramatically unwrapping his captive. Even before its fleshy torso was exposed, its odiferous markings wafted outward. The cover was thrown away, the five-eyed hybrid unveiled.

The Empress was not fooled. But her colony was. In that moment before she could muster her army or issue a new command to her mass, Lysis ended the charade.

"But you shall not have him!"

Ferrus Eviscamir unsheathed and sliced. The five-eyed head left its plinth, accepted by a floor of black muck. Gouts of white blood sprayed, showering Lord Lysis and his extended sword.

Then the intended chaos began.

Sounds of screeching, insane clicking, and leg scratching. The hybrid army's symphony lost harmony. From the crest of hopefulness to the trough of desperation, the army maddened. In an instant, their valued treasure was gone. Dissonance reigned as thousands of soldiers stormed the bogs, ruled by frenzy, not strategy.

The behemoth back peddled hastily. The Empress was swallowed by her legion's advancing fury. She kept her eyes on Lysis as she was conducted off the causeway. She emerged again in the distance, her behemoth was lost in the muddle. She flew now. Four wings raised her aloft, each spanning twice her height. So fast did they vibrate, they could not be seen discretely. Strong and controlled, she hovered in place at length. From within the center of her six regiments, she prepared to command her army, assuming she could regain control of her western regiments.

One third of her army had been lured into the bogs... and they were met...

ECHO WAS RECLUSIVE again. His isolation did not make him safer, but it may have helped the others. A feminine voice called to her prey, from within his own mind, "*My minion comes to retrieve you, scion.*"

Echo pleaded, "*I am not the king you seek.*"

"*Who are you, then?*"

"*Who am I?*" He repeated the Empress's question. "*I am...,*" then some other entity from inside him intruded, "*I am hers.*"

The Foundling Lord was confused. It was if he was interrupting a conversation between two aliens. Why was he in the middle of this? *What am I?*

The Empress answered: "*You are mine.*"

"*I am your royal consort,*" the shadow within Echo said. He closed his eyes, trying to squeeze out the strange voice, to cease the mysterious dialogue. Then he envisioned a serpent-like behemoth swim behind his eyelids. Was that the entity inside him? Or did the creature come from without? His heart raced. Was he breathing? A pang of terror rippled from his chest.

She spoke: *"My centimani comes for you now."*

He replied on his own behalf: *"No, do not. I do not want you."*

His shadow-self contradicted, *"...but I do want you...."*

The Empress hovered before him. Iridescent tendrils snaked from her middle eyes. These reached toward his gaping mouth; worked their way down his throat. He choked with the ethereal cords swelling his stomach. Then searched for, then prickled his heart. He became subdued. His pulse settled.

Echo was compelled to gaze at her, constrained by the astral cords anchored to him. She had a plan for him. He had to follow, obey. Mesmerized, he tried to disregard the tickling feeling within his chest. He tried to grab the chains, but his attempts failed. He could not speak either, being spellbound.

The Empress only had to keep him there, trap him until her minion finished tunneling under the Land. Echo listened to her: *Do not worry. All you have to do is stay put...*

The Foundling moaned abhorrently.

Helen sensed her master was not well. "Ruhyn, what is Lord Echo doing?"

"Tough to tell. He is hiding among the rocks. His feelers are swaying all over. Clanlord Bryhan is nearby. He doesn't seem concerned, whatever the case."

"I am going to help."

"Should you? Can you wait? Watch your step..."

Bran addressed her, "Helen, you must turn back."

"Our Lord needs us. Let me check—"

"Echo insists."

Helen pleaded, "We cannot sit idle as he pains. We must do something."

"He is our master, and controls the Gray powers." A cold hand pressed on her shoulder. "We only serve. I will get you when he allows." Bryhan nudged her kindly.

She sighed as Ruhyn took her hand and led her away. "I am confused. I feel Echo needs help. But he claims not."

"Lords deal with a lot we know nothin' about. Some things you can't heal, or don't need healing at all." He saw he was not allaying her anxiety. His own dreams weighed heavily on his heart, and he used them to distract her. "I have a city I'd like to heal." Ruhyn's pipe whistled in his palm, harmonizing with his sighs. "I need to be getting' back."

Helen tried to envision Tonn. It had to have been reduced to rubble by the battle. "You will go back? It is ruined. Shouldn't you stay here?"

"Just dreamin', Helen. My fantasies help me carry on through the madness."

He must indeed be mad to believe he could rebuild his homeland; yet questioning his optimism made reality more depressing. It seemed the Ill Age was returning. Helen covered her face with her hands, silently reflecting on their dim future. She surveyed her head's surface with her hands. The bandage was crusty with dried blood. Then she massaged her pliant pelt draped over her shoulders, brought it to her nose, and drank in the familiar smells. If only she could remove the dressing. Perhaps she could see well enough with her right eye. She imagined herself wearing a mask. She may need one to protect herself and cover up her scars. She thought of the Outsiders' helmets.

Ruhyn asked, "What are you ponderin'?"

The image of his cat helm materialized: a marble mask, white with green veins, covered his chin. "I would like to see… feel rather…your face. To learn what you look like."

Ruhyn removed the faceless helm and visor. Then he removed the ceramic facemask underneath.

"You left part of it on." She touched his face. There was no seam between the scarred skin and smooth ironstone piece covering his mouthpiece. Helen gasped.

"So you learn'n my secret."

"How did your face become so smooth?"

"Scars 'r smoother than skin. The glass I blown when young didn't take kindly to my mouth. I experimented blowing slag—that's the glassy stuff left over from the iron and copper furnaces. Colorful stuff that was. When molten, it's like liquid stars, sparklin' and colored like meteoric rock. Some of it was quicksilver, I knew. You can make some beautiful greens and blues from the forge refuse. Took a while for metal poison'in to show, and then it be too late. Working with that slag turned some of my tissue green. My father managed to remove it with his tools. Saved me from poison's that would've been worse, he said. Scar tissue grew in white and smooth."

"Is that…your real skin?" She touched his hairless chin. "It's beautiful."

Ruhyn spat out a laugh, "Aye, coming from a blind

woman!"

"Why hide it?"

He sighed. "Well skin didn't fix itself like glass does. My face scares all sorts of folk. You alone may think that my hairless face is more beauteous than a bearded chin."

"Well, it feels natural."

"Perhaps, but it doesn't look well. Seen me'self in a reflection. My face is too white, and the scars look veined like rock. During the Ill Age, Clanlord Kaiyn took his Legion of men searchin' for all the abducted women." He reflected for a moment then continued, "Back then, donnin' helmets was a tradition. Grovel Tonn inspired many with his helmets made to look like exotic land beasts."

"You were a warrior?"

"No. I was just a young glassmaker tryin' to keep folk from runnin' away from me. Understand there wasn't much order after the cataclysm. Kaiyn's Legion never came back, as you know. An' real mutants roamed about. For years I just kept away, hanging out in the mines. Some survivors went headin' to the Keep. Those stayed avoided me. My face scared 'em. They fear'd me a demon. Or, if they knew me as human, they fear'd I was contagious. Some urchins weren't afraid. Saw me as a leader, thinkin' my mask was royal. Started following me around. The pack members masked themselves to match my lead."

Burdon's kindling brand moved about the chamber, around Ruhyn and Helen. She was beginning to welcome his incessant cleansing rituals, and welcomed the scent of sage.

The heat trail suddenly stopped. The smoke dissipated. "Is that when Burden and you met?"

Ruhyn waited for his captain to meander out of earshot. "Burden was a lone wolf at first. Until he met a girl. Callin' herself Sunflare, she did. Her real name she hid, like I hide my true face. He called her Sunny for short."

"What happened to her?"

She heard the sound of the metal rolling steadfastly in his palm. She had made him nervous. Had she been more secure in herself, she would have understood that his habit was based from the demands of crafting glass symmetrically. His compulsion to fidget was not directly tied to her questioning.

"Been no proper weddings since the Ill Age. Still, he and her wanted to mark their courtship before Tonn's ancestors. They went to our Clan's sacred Tomb to do so. Under the Commons. Kohl, who often lurked there, was asked to witness. It was he who came to get help. A serpent had attacked 'em, he said—"

"White serpents? Like the one Bryhan's slew for his armor?"

"The same. Those snakes had been rare before the Grays came. Clanlord Kaiyn slayed a few. Gave his Sons their armor." Helen quietly acknowledged the fact that Bryhan had had a brother. There was much she did not know about her companions. "On that day, we learned that the snakes had become plentiful. They were comin' from somewhere from down below the mines, 'neath our tombs. An' we learned that they fed on blood."

Helena hugged herself. "Is that why he burns himself whenever he smudged? To hide the pain of Sunny?"

"Aye. Sometimes cleanin' with water only goes so far'. Some pain is rooted to the soul. Wash it, you may, but it'll just regenerate. Can't quench some fires." Ruhyn twirled his pipe faster. "So my pack rescued Burden. Took the lot of us to get the serpent to retreat. It took Sunny's corpse with it into the darkness. Burden joined us then, needin' be part of a community to survive. Teamed up with my group, we combed the mines and learned where the snakes—"

"Wyverns?"

"Yes. Wyverns. Ole' Whitebeard called them dragon larvae or snakes. They come from the same depths as the chromanti. All the shakin' of the earth during the cataclysms of the Ill Age shifted the Land. Ancient portals emerged into our tombs o' Tonn, beyond which be some otherworldly hell."

Their conversation was upstaged by the trembling of the earth.

Burden raised his ear from being pressed against rock, "Devils come."

Again the ground rumbled. The vibrations lingered longer. Sounds of dislodged rocks resonated. Instead of fading, the noise persisted: the enemy was close. Dust fell from the stalactites onto Helen's skin. Startled, she reached out, stumbling for a safer spot. Ruhyn caught her. Her white hair and bandages molded to his bending elbow, his exposed arm felt warm the instant her cheek compressed against it.

She asked, "What do...," the shuddering floor

interrupted, "...you see?"

Ruhyn's embrace confined her. She could feel him rotating his head, scanning the interior. Sand sprinkled onto them. Grit tumbled through her bandages. She flinched. He said, "I need to let you go. Something comes."

Left alone, Helen shivered. She imagined Ruhyn holding his metal staff as a spear, poised to strike. Another puff of dust crawled into Helen's nose. She coughed. She shook continuously as the earth vibrated, as if a thousand worms nibbled under the hard surface; bracing herself, she anchored her hands on the dry stone.

"Hide as best you can," Ruhyn yelled to her. He charged his pipe with lantern oil. "The first through that hole will burn." Ruhyn lit the opposite end, so his weapon transformed into a lengthy torch.

Hugging the stone, searching for a crevice, Helen found a crawlspace refuge. Wedged between two sandstone slabs, she curled up in a bed of golem seeds. Her hands explored their little shapes. Quaking made her drop the expired homunculi shells. She reached for support. The stone trembled beneath her hands; it grew warm. Then it became pliant, and felt more like a large callus than it did rock. *The earth is becoming animated*, she determined. Helen wondered briefly on the Doctor's existence, being that he was the only earthen elemental she knew. She did not realize that the ancient golem seeds among which she rested, the materials drawn on for geomancy, were the same type of energy fueling the colossal crawler that wrapped the Hollow's exterior.

Scratching reverberated everywhere. Beside her, the rock shifted, cracked, and oozed a metallic smelling, viscous liquid that wetted her dress. Blood? Something outside was digging into the chamber. What monstrosity could have climbed so high?

The men had focused on the threshold. It was, they had ascertained, the most vulnerable opening. They had expected clarion calls, and hybrids made of chitin; these did not come. Instead, a single entity breached the Hollow, one too big to enter by any threshold for bipeds or quadrupeds: the behemal centimani.

Dust storms clotted the lanterns, their flames did little but illume turbid clouds. Darkness poured into the Hollow. Then the putrid rank of injured flesh infused the chamber. They saw only a giant, frilled tongue. It was too dark to identify a face, if there was one. Despite being a single body, a chorus of screeching came from its countless agglomerated beaks and human faces.

Then Helen heard the din of battle: the roar of Ruhyn's flaming stave, the swish of Bryhan's spear, and the thunk of Burden's hammer. Only Echo did not attack. The Gray Lord shied away from the behemoth's groping wrath. He was still distracted, wrestling personal demons.

"I am calling to her as much as she is to me," the voice within him spoke.

Echo held his head. *"You are a stranger in my mind...my body. What is your name?"*

No answer.

"Who are you?"

The hybrid lord slapped his torso and thorax, then he scraped the transition from skin to chitin, which delaminated more. Ghostly visages emerged of his future self from under the chitin shingles. His singular self was being sundered…

"I am a scion… I am you…"

"Echo?" Helen yelled. "The stone is turning to flesh." Her human companions were not able to inspect this sorcery. The immediate threat of the writhing behemoth commanded their attention.

Echo did not answer his curer.

Nor could the others, engaged as they were with the many-bodied creature. It recoiled, flapping about the chamber, its hands groping the cavernous Hollow. Every contact point succumbed to the Empresses' sorcery, the fluids of the creature turning mineral to cytoplasm.

A moment of clarity enabled the men to see the monstrosity: a giant hybrid born from experiment, not nature. It was very wide; if Bryhan, Ruhyn, and Burden grabbed hands in a circle, they would not have been able to surround its waist. Its length was not determinable, since only a portion penetrated the Hollow.

Burden struggled. Four arms tugged at his weapons, a face gnawed his left forearm, as antennae probed his body, and insectan pincers locked about his right leg.

Ruhyn discharged his blowpipe, and a length of vaporized oil, burning bright, shot toward the beast. Incendiary breath ignited it. The faces under the hair screeched terrible cries of pain.

I can stop this. She only wants me, Echo thought to himself. Striding past his curer, he tried to call out to her, yet his throat was still inoperable. The Empress affected him still. She allowed him to move, but only toward the creature.

Helen sensed her Lord's presence. His anxiety. She tried to grab him but missed. "Lord, do not go!" She searched blindly, "Bran, are you there? Can you see him? Help!"

Echo walked toward the conflagration, entranced.

Bryhan shouted "Lord!" The call did not bring his lord back to reality, so the Guard intervened by chasing after him. Burden followed in turn. Tumorous limbs grabbed for them. Hammer and spear lashed out, detaching smoldering appendages. Creamy ichor splattered Helen. Was it Echo's? Bran's? Suddenly, Helen vomited. Steaming bile lurched from her throat. She immediately knew that Echo or Bryhan was hurt. Indeed, Bryhan had been incapacitated, falling alongside his stave as he shielded Echo. Alien arms compressed him against the beast. He did not realized his Lord intended to be taken…

"Helena?"

"Lord?" She responded aloud, though his voice had come from within her. "Are you near me? Do you bleed?'

"I speak telepathically. It takes a long time to build such a pathway, especially when no blood is shared. I do not like to mindspeak this way. But I must. With haste. I am poisoned. My body corrupt. It is over…I must end this…"

"No!" Helen tore at her bandage. It unwrapped partially. The bloody rag refused to be discarded. Scabs adhered it to her white hair. Her right eye was uncovered regardless. From it, she saw flashes of fire, bursts of smoke, and silhouettes of flickering appendages cast onto vaporized dirt.

Echo was close. She could smell him. He had to be about somewhere. Then she saw him atop the creature. Was he riding it?

"...I leave you..."

She did not notice the behemoth's fingers until they were on her. She was too weak to fight. By submitting, at least she would go with her lord. Perhaps she could find a way to serve him.

"Helen!" Ruhyn tried to release the limbs holding her tight, prying his pipe under the net of sinew. The centimani curled about Ruhyn. He was pulled into the mass, collapsing face down, clutching Helen's legs. Feathered talons wrapped about him, and compacted him against Helen. He was held in place.

The Hollow was emptied.

The behemoth snaked down the column. Then it retreated, swimming the sea of melancholy, cautious not to drown its living treasure under black oil. It crawled onto the Underworld shore, departing through the tunnel which it bored. The band was taken away from the Keep, away from the battle in the moat. Toward the unknown...

Then Echo mind-spoke a cryptic, final command, *"Helena...Bran...you are dismissed..."*

THE SUN SET beyond the Keep's zenith, casting a mountainous shadow onto the battlefield, creeping faster and faster over the bogs. A few stray clouds ventured between Land and Sky to further mottle the frontline of the carnage. Here, the Empress's westernmost two regiments had gone berserk, storming the black moat, having believed that Lysis had destroyed their prize. They rushed to him enraged.

The marsh surface swelled as they entered. White-veined larvalwyrmen threaded the frothy liquid, wrapping the angular limbs of frenzied chromanti. The water roiled with the splashes of the drowning. The turmoil released a miasma of atomized tar, black water, and white blood.

These creatures may have been immeasurably loyal to their empress, but they were prone to panic and illusions. More could be lured away from her control. Lord Lysis continued to play on this fear. He would use the mounting mist of death rising from the bog as his medium. Remaining seated on the once-Queen, he drew his weapon.

Ferrus Eviscamir leapt from left to right hand, racing around its master's back. Each swath birthed visages in the black fog, catalyzing fear in the enemy. Lysis shaped it to reflect their thoughts: ghosts of their decapitated consort. They feared handling the captives they had brought in cages, so he hypnotized them. They visualized their companions splitting into two Spawnen. Phantom hybrids morphed into their components: headless chepris rode upon crippled slyphin; torso-less chromanti seizured, unable to upright themselves; legless humans crawled awkwardly off balance.

Out of sight behind the shuttered South Gate, curers gathered orderly around the Pyre feeding their Lord's sorcery. Without it, his spells would falter and the larvalwyrmen would become still. His regiment of curators stoked the fire and drew upon their flags which, on the astral plane, burned as bright as the main blaze. It empowered him at great cost. The curators' strength waned. Creating art constantly, and offering it as fast, had drained their minds. They had consumed all the paper in the Keep and now scavenged fabric to paint. Moreover, they depleted their supply of ink. Hence the scullery was raided: soups, butter, and pickle brine served as paints. They drew pictures. Immolated them. Drew again. Still their Lord demanded more. He did not ask or instruct. He just took the energy he needed and expected the fire to be maintained. So it was. His necromancy cost them their color. Brunette hairs faded to white. Black to gray. Skin paled and desiccated, having aged prematurely. Cheeks sunk inward. A great measure of beauty had left them, taken directly by Lysis who funneled the energy toward all those who had his *lapis elixir* running in their veins.

"Grave, clear the bogs." Lysis commanded.

The Doctor left the causeway as his master cast magic. Mud dripped from his apron. Slick oil stained his arms. A mature, multi-segmented larvalwyrmen emerged at his side. He mounted it and glided like a snake over the bog's surface. His mobility was an overpowering competitive advantage.

The enemy was so encumbered they appeared

comatose: coated with heavy black oil; sunken into viscous slime; wrapped by leathery larvalwyrmen. The wyrms threaded the chromanti with unearthed skeletons from the under bog. It was as if the thousands Grave had murdered during the Ill Age had resurfaced. These grotesqueries were not like the members of the Gray Horde; these were just exhumed bones threaded by the white-blooded wyrms. Most hybrids attempted to move. Extended, springing, locust legs jolted them up. Fast movement was only met with stronger resistance. So to move efficiently, those ensnared had to crawl slowly.

Wielding *Ferrus Hewnmaw*, the Doctor waded forward to mete out death, cleaving legs, antennae, and arms. Chitin fractured under his ax blows. Wherever the Doctor's weapon sang, victims lost blood, color, and soul while turning into glass. Transparent bodies fell, their husks turned to brittle crystal by *Hewnmaw's* powers. Shards of these glass hybrids shattered. The chromantaur soldiers failed in the tumultuous froth of war. White blood flowed atop the bog water like molten fat. Layers of the freshly killed joined the immersed, decomposed bodies of the mature dead. Accordingly, the water level rose. The causeway became thinner and thinner as the bloody stew lapped the land bridge.

The moat and causeway fell under Grave's control.

The enemy soldiers of the Southwest and Northwest regiments of the enemy were nearly depleted. Only their magical standard bearers remained, being less susceptible to Lysis' tricks. Six bands of the chepri, with their enslaved slyphin and their cages of red-blooded fodder, were equidistantly spread from the Empress. The closest was the Northwest regiment's flag, near the shoreline. Grave surmised this group was rearranging the cages of humans, rocs, and elder insects. Imprisoned as they were, they could not defend themselves as the chepri walked about, cutting them with a flaying knife.

The Doctor hurled several vials containing diseased, blue blood. One woman, already cut, reached into the pool, her arms straining through the bone bars. She was desperate, grabbing to procure a chemical that may help. She retrieved a vial with it the cork removed, and the blue liquid coursed over her bleeding arms. She was turned to stone. The chepri had never seen such a reaction. The red blood of the slaves was not known to petrify to them, yet suddenly the pool of blood meant to fuel the Empress was calcifying. The alchemy was not perfect, but the distraction was sufficient to cease the enemy's spell casting from this regiment. *"Lord, she draws on their blood for her sorcery. I can stop—"*

"Stay here." Lysis commanded. He was already eyeing the Empress. She floated a half mile away at the center of her army. Energy from her remaining pyres, the chepris' pennons, streamed toward her. *"Her sorcery will not last. Her vessels of energy are not hers to keep. Protect the bogs. It is time I approach the Empress directly."*

Lord Lysis left the causeway toward the Gray Orchard wherein stood the nearest regiment's standard bearer, one of the sylphin-riding, ant-headed chepri. The marsh adjacent to the bogs had become true flesh, assuming the look of a black-veined corpse. He rode over this cytoplasm, infiltrated the Empress's ranks on the south bank where his impaled Horde had arisen amongst the hybrid militia. This regiment had overcome Lysis' ruse only to be surprised by the skeletons and manikins amongst them. Hundreds of Lysis' Horde jumped into action, springing from crucifixes and dropping from stanchions.

This enemy was nearly routed until the Empress worked her magic. The tide of battle turned fast. The bodies of Lysis' Horde could not think for themselves. They had to be controlled like puppets. Until the Empress granted them true, independent life. She transmuted the Gray Horde's inorganic bodies into organic tissue. White ichor exuded from their bodies. Lungless manikins began to breathe. The soulless art forms experienced pain for the first time, without any way to comprehend emotion. The more manikins she turned alive, the less Lysis could possess. Unless he could get to their hearts since, as the Doctor professed with The Rule of Animation, he could not control their minds directly. Yet these manikins had been granted life without hearts. They were strange, insane monstrosities. The Horde also comprised fleshless skeletons, which fared no better, their hearts having disappeared through decay. The heartless Horde flailed about senselessly. The enemy assigned one soldier per limb, and one for the head, to form star shaped patterns; they quartered most. Poised, the cavalry turned to greet the mounted Lord Lysis.

The once-Queen navigated pools of pitch adjacent the Orchard. Lysis cut down his own confused ranks as well as the enemy as he ploughed through the Gray Orchard. Appendages flew: stripped legs, shell armor, pliant wooden arms, sun bleached skulls, eyeless, noseless heads. A hundred yards separated them from a wall of chromanti lancers. The once-Queen towered over the soldiers composing it, meaning to scale it and meet the Empress. Before they met, a dozen hybrid drones jumped from behind the barrier, spurred by their great locust legs. Airborne, they flew in great arcs. They targeted their pikes, pointing them downward, and fell toward their lone adversary. The once-Queen reared. Lysis held on. His warrior skills were not needed yet. His eldritch steed fought better while moving. He chose to save his strength and charge.

His mount's elephantine incisors swept back and forth. Dashing the hopping chromanti aside. Three struck her massive form with spears. Two of these shattered. The last impaled her abdomen. This did not slow her; she was undead, and a puncture to her exoskeleton did little to drain what empowered her. She continued her advance with the broken handle planted in her side.

Still the hybrids moved to surround them. The once-Queen pushed the enemies away with her lengthy limbs, antennae, and tusks. Moving forward, she crawled atop any that fell. Her smaller mandibles snapped fast to cleave off appendages. In less than two minutes, the first dozen attackers spasmed, curled, and contorted.

Another dozen chromanti launched from behind the shield wall. They descended to their deaths as the first wave had. The infantry line stepped forward, lances lowered. The once-Queen darted to meet them. Rampant, she collided. Intent on scaling the row, she angled herself and climbed over the smaller foe.

Behind the main line, the entire South Regiment turned. They motioned to swarm. If Lysis stayed here, he would certainly be buried. Even as Lysis dismounted, hundreds enveloped them in a cage of bodies. With haste, the skeletal lord slashed with *Ferrus Eviscamir* to carve out a path toward the enemy's leader and the humans she enslaved. He left the once-Queen to screen the drones. She commanded attention. The chromanti could not harm her, being that she was already dead, but they could immobilize her. They networked themselves into a seamless mass.

Meanwhile, her master headed toward the regiment's standard. The chepri was only twenty yards away riding its sylphin. Its pennant burned brilliant white. Before he reached this standard-bearer, Lysis was met by scrambling lancers. *Ferrus Eviscamir* deflected a shaft aimed at his face. He sidestepped. Mutilated a foe. He jumped over another lance, and sliced both left legs from a chromantaur. It toppled over and struck another. Carcasses fell upon carcasses. None could match his speed. Circuitously he moved forward.

A flying spear shot toward Lysis. He rolled closer to the chepri. Three more shafts flew. One skewered the Lord, pinning him to sodden earth-turned-flesh. The force shot *Ferrus Eviscamir* from his hands. White blood gushed from his ribcage. The chromanti engulfed him. His legs sprawled. His arms taken either direction. Two managed to grab his horned head.

The eagle-headed slyphin prowled toward him. The chepri rider meant to inspect the vulnerable Lord. The hybrid was naïve to believe that the being before him lacked power. The Empress was not accustomed to Lysis' style of sorcery; her subordinate sorcerers were even less prepared. The pennant blazed white in the astral plane, though the chepri could not *see* it. A current from it flowed toward the Empress and amplified her control over the regiment. Lysis did not need to bring his resources with him to battle; he would pirate their energy. The standard bearer could not *see* the skeletal lord redirecting its fire. Weakening the connection to the Empress, it strengthened Lord Lysis, almost as if he had walked into his own Pyre. The Empress tried to reclaim the energy, but could not. His aura burned brightly. Hers dimmed. Exhausted of energy, the standard spontaneously combusted. Sylphin and rider likewise erupted in real flames.

Lysis remained ensnared within the six chromanti. His bones glowed white-hot. His *lapis elixir* now bled through his wounds, and mingled with his captors' grapple locks. He waited patiently. His stamina was greater than these six soldiers, and he hoped to bait the Empress closer.

But she never approached.

He directed his blood to flow onto, into, the enemy. Rivulets of his white blood defied gravity, streamed into their wounds, their chitin joints, and their mouths and noses. It would not react with their white ichor, but it would still swell their veins, pool in their skulls. Soon their ears wept white tears. Blood surged into the chromanti. The insectan hybrids stubbornly held as their skulls become cysts. Their Empress had commanded they hold Lysis; they did—even as their heads pressurized, cracked and exploded. They fell, headless, into the dirt.

Lysis stood, retrieved his sword. Yet he was not done with the six. He seized their hearts and souls, raised them. He set them upon their own ranks that swarmed the once-Queen. Headless, undead chromanti sought to free the Lord's mount, mutilating their own kind. Each converted hybrid created a site of chaos. An alien among them of like form. The organized ranks crumbled as they turned upon each other. Antennae working overtime scanning for familiar blood. Allegiances no longer could be trusted by scent or body shape.

He could see the Empress and her rearguard sorcerers preparing the pit from which she arrived. The Lord advanced toward his royal enemy. A regiment of her cavalry lay between. He would not reach her in time to stop her next conjuration.

The Empress's sorcery demanded sacrifice, and she had many ready: nine and one hundred fathers; thirty-nine and one hundred mothers; their verdant, helpless children. Lord Lysis was not their steward by rite, but he would try to save them regardless. If only he could have reached them. The roc cages were emptied into the pit. The slaughtering of the prisoners began.

A translucent, ruby-tinted pall floated from the heap. This vaporized blood ascended skyward, coalesced into clouds. The Empresses' glorious, buzzing wings bellowed it westward. Over the marshes. Up, over the mountainous scree of the Chromlechon. Higher than the ramparts along South Gate. It blotted out the hot sun. It cast sweeping swathes of maroon atop a battlefield already mottled with darkening gore.

The Empress imparted life to the blood cloud. The impregnated fog morphed in anguish, assuming the shape of tormented souls from which it derived. They became hyper-ventilating phantasms familiarizing themselves with death. Vaporous faces vomited scarlet plumes; they breathed heavily, panic laden. Virtual veins swelled in their crunched foreheads, across swollen purple lips. Blood vessels outgrew the illusions from which they sprang. Once realized, the arterial tentacles jellied, and grew into red threads of elastic lightning.

Emotions congealed and showered the Chromlechon courtyard in thick crimson clots. Red rain sizzled in the fire, dousing Lysis' retinue. Bloody fingers descended from the Sky, curling like searching-vines for support. Twirling. Groping. Until they found the weary curators. The suspended arteries wrapped around their supple necks, then levitated. The curers dangled like ornaments. Lysis' flags were soiled. Seventeen fell, extinguished. Still it rained blood. Wetted, the Pyre coughed.

Grave alerted, *"Lord, her clouds attack your Pyre!"*

Lysis hardly needed the warning. The assault had already drained his strength and called his attention. He responded by directing his pyre-sprites to land along the dangling arteries, self-assembling into lines. As individuals, they could not harm the fleshy filaments. Their collective presence localized their Lord's power, connecting the monstrosities to him. Score upon scores of his receptors were aligned and waiting as more joined. Most fluttered their kindling wings so that they scintillated orange.

Lysis raised *Ferrus Eviscamir* over his head. Its tip oriented toward his Pyre. He spat arcane speech from his white-hot skull. Arcs of lightening leapt from his horned crown, feeding the sword. Charged, the magical blade blazed blue.

Thunder clapped. All basked in the glory of a blooming, white screen that veiled Lord Lysis. Then all shuddered in the unavoidable, overpowering shockwave emanating from him. For an instant, a circuit had connected the Lord to his papyrus minions. Electricity flowed. Lightning dissipated the blood clouds.

The curators were released from the disintegrating phantom gallows. Their dead bodies dropped suddenly. Impotent arteries fell, incandescent. Burning segmented whips extinguished as they collapsed.

Puffs of smoke drifted about. The battlefield quieted.

The tide had turned.

The Empress issued a singular, sudden order. Her word transmitted as a ghostly whisper from her pursed mouth, and as faint as it may have been, it resonated on every antennae left on the battlefield. The Empress's order was her final one. Abruptly, she turned away from the setting sun. She flew away with haste eastward, toward the striped mountains of Tonn.

Lysis could feel her absence. At once, the tug-of-war for her energy suddenly ceased. The thrill of a day's battle receded. Too quickly.

"Something is not right." Grave said. *"She is leaving. Why would she abandon her army?"*

The disowned chromanti executed her final command:

they massacred the remaining captives. None could be rescued. There would be no dryadic humans alive to tell tales of the strange land from whence they came. No more fathers. No mothers. No children. Nor would there be any elders to replenish the extinct species. No humans or elders alive for Grave to study in his Theater.

The sun sank behind the Chromlechon now. The enemy had come at dawn and left at dusk.

"Grave, we underestimated her." Lysis tried to mindspeak to his fellow Gray to no avail: no response. *"Echo has been taken."*

The Lord was faced with several choices: one, go under the Keep to save Echo; two, follow the Empress; or three, fight her army. He had faced similar choices at the end of the Ill Age, in which he saved Echo in the Underworld. His priorities were clear. Lysis descended under the Keep.

IV: The Final Imago Emerges from Tonn Tomb

Ruhyn's arm draped across Helen's ribcage. They were compressed under the behemoth's interlocking extremities. Immobilized, they moved with their vessel as if they lay on a raft, plunging through white-foamed rapids. However, they were underground. Their senses were obscured. Darkness precluded sight. Confinement prohibited reaching out to feel beyond. Inharmonious rumbling overwhelmed hearing. A scent that approximated pungent flesh evoked memories of when Helen performed the lesser duties of a novice curator, cleaning the Doctor's Theater after his demonstrations.

Foreign, slick skin and hairs blocked Helen's face such that her lips had to suck air through a bristly network. She was short of breath, confused. Had she been eaten by the monster?

Transported for hours, she had become numb. She blacked out for a time. Her lids struggled to re-open. Were they open already? Her sockets ached. She longed to see something again. Her last memorable visions replayed themselves, less sharp than her dreams and memories: splotches of orange fire, blurred white flashes, and limned silhouettes of rocks.

Helen's muscles ached. She could not feel her left leg. It should still be there. How long they undulated beneath the earth, she had no idea. Bereft of her senses, she was unable to do anything but dream or hallucinate. The hands that held her were no longer from the behemoth. Now corpse arms held her; sooty, blackened hands, dragging her down into the dark bowels of the earth. She was dead too. And more bloated bodies floated beside her.

Helen knew where she was now. Under the bogs she hated. Phosphorescent jelly bodies swam by. Ancient, translucent fossils with lengthy filaments swayed in invisible currents, with gaping maws mouthing obscure words. She must be dreaming. Had her eyes not been injured? The visions were too detailed to be real. Her mind's eye fooled her. Dreaming or not, she was cold. The sinew straps that held her radiated little heat. In contrast, Ruhyn's arm compressed to her belly was warm enough to keep her blood flowing. Without him, she would have succumbed to the cold. Instead she managed to maintain delirium.

Helena? The voice came from behind her. Her burnt mother and father held her now. She could feel something on her back. Jaws, opening and closing, pressed against the nape of her neck. Their decaying arms wrapped about her.

Helen, I will protect you! Her father's ghost avowed, hugging her so she could not break free, dragging her into the Underworld. Then her captors, and she, were covered in a cloud of pungent ash. Her parents were silenced. The darkness leeched their ghosts away.

A luminous rag doll floated out of the obscurity. Its marble eyes, glossy and tear coated, reflected the unnatural glow of the other phantoms. It reached for the ribbon in her hair and unraveled it. So the braid unfurled…and a ribbon of silk was freed. As the doll pulled away with the current, Sharon's effigy emerged, her curly hair singed, kindling at the tips. Plumes of sparkling ash trailed her buoyant arms.

Their eyes met. Sharon's ghost mouthed silent words.

Helen struggled to understand.

"I'll save you…," Sharon seemed to say, petting the pelt still mantled to Helen's shoulders. Sharon's ghost seemed to impart life into the hide, and it began to move like a living cat. Helen felt the cat paw at her bandages that flapped with the same tempo of her host's undulating. As the behemoth wormed its way under the earth, her head lurched and withdrew accordingly, ever limited in motion by monstrous, fleshy cilia. Yet the torn flag would not leave her. It no longer covered her eyes. Unfurled, it was still bound to her, entwined with her locks. Glued with scabs to her scalp. Her standard had become one of her charms.

Her other relics floated before, tied to her white braids, anchored to her head, yet free from the net of appendages. Knots of silk ribbons unraveled in the dark current. Ceramic beads let loose. Drifted away. The relics disappeared from view instantly. How fast must she be moving? Alas, she could not reach out to retrieve them. The golem husk hung on. The homunculus shell assumed the appearance of a fruit dangling from a bough, the jelly endocarp sprouting embryonic fingers that held fast to her hair. The stillborn ghost held a braid tightly, as if it were an umbilical cord. It cried.

A blinding white light erased this horrific vision.

Helen felt a cessation of movement.

A hybrid's silhouette approached. It bent over her to inspect. Eerie light crawled across its masculine face. Its head was slightly different than Echo's had been. This face was softer, more refined. Beautiful, but alien.

Then a second face appeared, as angelic, but feminine. The pair looked down upon her.

The female stared with detached curiosity. That creature thought Helen was pathetic.

In the male, she saw relief, betrayal, and guilt. Helen's lips quivered too much to speak. Yet, she recognized him. It was Echo. His effigy smiled, yet a hint of corruption in his countenance made her doubt. Was it really Echo? Had he transformed? Or was this an imposter?

Helen's cat spirit hissed a warning.

Her Lord and his alien mate vaporized. Her fantastical visions departed under the weight of real darkness. She became fully awake, aware that she was bound to some monstrosity within the Underworld. Beneath the bogs…

BRYHAN'S IRON SHAFT pressed against his chest. Immobilized, he surveyed the cavernous crypt with his *sight*. The behemoth had entered the cave to his right. Its geomancy had turned the stone it touched into flesh. It had brought life to a chamber dedicated to Tonn's dead. Now the centimani lay still.

Nearby, Burden wriggled within the network of appendages. The ram-helmed miner was unable to see anything. He would not know that the undead guardian of Echo observed his struggles. For a period, Burden thrashed madly. His anger intensified to a lithium red. His soul sparked as it contacted the creature's crimson aura. Uncleanliness crawled over him. Eventually, fatigue prevailed. His spirit dimmed again, and he was forced to rest. He sniffed the air and became hopeful. Scents of the environment were diffusing through the rank of the behemoth. The chamber smelled of smoke. Stone. Recognizing his home Tonn, Burden's aura suddenly calmed; he fell asleep.

The behemoth had stopped beside the extinguished hearth of giant crystals, the centerpiece of the Tomb. A furlong beneath the vaulted alabaster stalactites, Bryhan's mummified ancestor Clan Lords were encased in tincal-glass coffins. Bryhan could hear echoes of Doctor Grave codify the Rules of Relics: souls of artisans were encased with their art. How better to sanctify the bond than to create art from the dead Lords, Ladies, Lordsons, Sons, and Daughters? Buried here were Tonn's Craft Lords too: master kiln builders, colliers, miners, and alchemists, even great grandfathers who had completed the underground artery connecting the limestone quarries of Calx Mountains to the foundation of the sandstone mines of the Arenites. Absent were Bryhan's brother, Lordson Taiyn who was lost in the Land's gorge to a Gallwraith attack, and his parents, Lady Aleece and Clanlord Kaiyn who were lost in the bogs.

Unlike soft glass, made solely from Arenites' base sandstone, these sarcophagi would not melt in wood furnaces. Working tincal-glass required athanors fed with purified charcoal, which burned hotter than raw wood. Only by blending the powders with the finest silicates, atop the hottest fire, could they produce such resilient glass. The process was so hot that most colored minerals burned away, rendering it clear as the finest jewelry. It did not expand or crack in common man's fire. The secret craft had been employed to preserve their finest leaders. Now the souls of the dead Lords stared from within these faceted pillars at the reanimated Son of Clanlord Kaiyn Tonn. Bryhan recalled how they ignited the mineral fonts in the Hearth every Winter's Solstice. Each had burned brilliantly: golden, rock-salt fire; lilac-pink potash flames; grass-greens blazes of copper ore. These fonts were cold now, but ethereal limelight seemed to emanate flickers of past blazes.

The royal ghosts whispered, *"Son Bryhan. You have returned."*

Bran had to find Echo, not be lured into the past by engaging his ancestors. He focused his undead eyes on the centimani's coiled form. It was a listless heap. The only vestige of life it showed was an occasional spasm. He eventually spotted two human bodies compressed to its side: Helen and Ruhyn. Their auras still burned feverishly; they were alive. Then he looked toward the tusked anterior of the creature. There he spotted his master.

Echo swayed prostrate, rocking in slow motion. His back arched while his thorax and legs cradled the behemoth. A blanket of his old self delaminated. Sections of exoskeleton strained and peeled, extending lengths of translucent, gelatinous slime between his previous and final imago. The albuminous adhesive crackled. For every inch of new flesh exposed, an inch of past was discarded.

"Lord!" Bryhan called out, his lethargy dissipated as he was spurred to action. *"You molt!"* Desperate, he worked to free himself. He could not break free.

The Gray Lord acknowledged his guard with a sudden, dismissive glance.

As quickly as Bryhan's resurgence had grown, his energy waned again. White ichor drained from Bryhan's heart. *"No. I still serve you—"*

Bryhan opened his mouth to speak, but was too weak. He tried to mindspeak, but his words dissolved in the ether. The *lapis elixir* empowering him was receding. His master was withdrawing his blood. His heart slowed. With each thrust his master advanced, Bryhan's strength decremented. He realized then that Echo was the only one of the original party not constrained by the beast. In fact, he was on top of it. His arms grasped two large antennae at the forefront of the centimani. He had ridden it. Echo had steered it here. Was he a traitor?

The behemoth's wriggling appendages disrobed the skin from Echo. Two dozen hands pulled the old shell away. The new imago emerged from the sticky shed skin.

Suddenly, a white flare illuminated the chamber from above. The chamber's ceiling transmuted into flesh. The stalagmites above the crystal sarcophagi glowed. Stone pillars fluidized, melting into liquid strands that rippled away from a central source. Alien sorcery mutated the minerals like none ever mastered within Tonn. Was the brilliant, white moon descending?

Angelic white wings eased the Empress to the ground. She landed as elegantly as a butterfly, while above the elastic once-stone sealed the ceiling's laceration. Her antennae quivered. She sensed her own pheromones already present here. Head scanning, she searched. Echo's aura burned whiter, more intense than before. It burned like hers. She went to him.

Extending a lithe arm to her mate, she pronounced, "Welcome, my consort." She spoke in a foreign tongue akin to the arcane language the Doctor used during his rites. The being that emerged was a twin of Echo, except its body burned as an otherworldly blaze. This halo matched that of the female who was helping him gain his footing.

Bryhan looked at his transformed master. Its bodily form was similar to that which was present prior to the transformation; but it was smoother now. White fleshy, skin blended from its chest into hard chitin with seamless grace. Its face was more mature, its cheeks more sunken. It had five eyes: three ebony ocelli sat in a triangle between the larger primary set. Beside the Empress, it was clearly of her kind. She was taller than the imago, and her graceful arms wrapped about him, leading it up onto his four legs. Her lips opened, "Call me Veneda."

The imago paused as her radiating aura washed over it, took its breath away. Looking up, it took in her physical beauty, which surpassed that of her shade: slender cheeks, alluring lashes, lustrous eyes brimming with rich, emotive fluid. Her presence compelled an introduction, which left it dumbfounded.

Who am I?

From behind, the vacated exuviate muttered, *"Echo..."*

That name was obsolete, given by Bryhan to a mysterious child rescued on a battlefield. That name was only fitting for its younger selves, its discarded imagoes. Presently, it had no name. Not until she anointed it. Her caress wiped the anxiety from its brow; left her soul-stain on its forehead which seeped into his mind.

"My transformation is complete. I am—"

"I name you Servandum. My royal mate." Wrapping her stole around him, she drew him close. Wings curled seductively about him.

Servandum let the Empress lead him away from his old self and the centimani carcass. His past selves had merely been looking for someone to order him. That quest never satisfied and often hurt others. Now, he was utterly relieved. No longer did he have to derive something for himself. He could now serve Veneda, free of the crushing worry of finding an elusive purpose. Within her blooming aura of beauty, Servandum was bathed in her purpose. He had found his goal. He was with his own kind. Another hybrid. *"I thought you meant to kill me. But you were trying to rescue me. I am yours."*

Her five eyes intimately aligned with his. The attraction was innate. His soul flared with hers. Her wet lips glided to his neck. Likewise, his mouth slid to her neck. Mandibles clasped, and they drank upon each other's white blood. Their hunger was mutual, and their behavior a symbiotic, euphoric vampirism. Blood and soul from the two united.

She embraced him, *"You no longer live with those who are diseased."*

"But?" His questioned, confused. Two decades of watching Lysis hunt down vile hybrids had taught him that the mutant creatures were sick and unnatural. *"The humans are the healthy, innocent ones. I...you... are products of dyscrasia. Aren't we hybrids the diseased?"*

She read his memories. Servandum's younger self had bled many men of ether, turning them gray. The being, known as Echo, had been a parasite. She saw how he had drained the color and soul from innocents uncontrollably, turning those who aided him into mad creatures. Then she saw a gradual peace emerge as he aged. A curer's hand had calmed him. Then this same Spawn nursed him, becoming medium of the creative forces he required. The she saw images of Sharon's death. *"Your mind is wracked with nervous energy. Your spirit is a tortured web of emotional knots born from ignorance."*

Servandum pleaded. *"How will I feed? Without a curer?"*

"My naïve consort, I will teach you," she said. *"No*

wonder your soul is wrought with anxiety. The ignorant have corrupted your thoughts. You...we... are not diseased, as the Spawnen would have you believe. Those red-bloods are insecure things who misunderstand how they evolved. Those that raised you are dangerously ill. Can you not see their red blood and souls? Nature will drive them to remix, to mate across species, consume another's flesh, and transform back into chromanti. " She gestured toward his and her aura, *"By many measures, we chromanti are healthier. The* lapis elixir *in our veins is eucrasiac.* "

Meanwhile, white ichor drained from Bryhan's heart. It would not be long until his powers were completely exhausted. Leveraging his spear, he contorted the arm-shackles. Crossed. Yanked. Pressed. With a desperate jolt, the binds gave precipitously. Free, he sprinted toward the pair. They were too far away. His heart would fail before he would reach them, so he prepared his weapon for flight. Letting loose the shaft, he cried, *"Strike true, Aleece!"* Then Bryhan crumbled.

Servandum would not have his mate skewered. He launched from the ground. His fresh wings were wide and powerful. Flying faster than the metal rod, he deflected the spear with an orthogonal strike. The being that had been Echo approached his former Guard.

Bryhan's corpse was motionless. His tethered soul said, *"You betray us! My Lord, I saw you atop her behemoth. You were free from its clutches. You controlled that thing. You are in league with it. With her!"*

"All these years I have been searching for my purpose

in a Land in which I do not belong. Now it…she…has finally been revealed. I must go with Empress Veneda. Indeed, it would be unnatural to ignore her. Yet as I depart, I do my best to honor your loyalty. I could have directed the behemoth a variety of directions away from the Keep. But I steered it here, to let you rest where you belong. With your ancestors." Servandum bent to pick up the Bryhan's corpse.

"Lord, what are you doing to my body?"

Servandum carried Bryhan to the Tomb's center. He collected Aleece's spear and staked it vertically into the ashen bed amongst the glass sarcophagi. Then he propped his old guard up in the bier, cradling his weapon. His distinctive lamellar armor sparkled

"At least one of Kaiyn's Sons will rest here."

"Echo, my Lord, I must…"

"I am Echo no longer. I am Servandum, Empress Veneda's mate."

"And who was I? I was a son to an adoring mother, whom I could not save from death. I was a son to a father, a Clanlord who saw more in my brother than me. And I was a guardian to you, who casts me aside…"

"Without you, Bran, I would have died on a battlefield, and many times since. You led and inspired others by your actions without seeking reward. You sought servitude rather than fame. You have been a quiet, loyal hero to your family. Now you are home. Here, even as one dead, you will inspire the Outsiders to be as noble. And you are free, for you have no obligation toward me."

The Son of Tonn acknowledged his ancestor's souls. His mother's soul. He was thankful to be home as much as he was sad to be relieved of duty. *"I am free."*

"We must go." Veneda ordered. She pointed toward the behemoth. "I'll need to draw upon its blood to open a gateway."

Servandum aided her in positioning the centimani for the Empress's sorcery. They directed the anterior toward the eastern exit, which led toward the mines beneath the Calx mountains. The rest of the behemoth had to be elongated linearly. Servandum inspected the creature as he nudged it. The humans were all unconscious. Burden. Ruhyn. Helena. All were alive. Servandum approached the blinded curator. Ruhyn was pinned chest down, his arm draped across Helena. He regarded the flag still loosely attached to her head. He tugged it free with a jerk, waking her. "This standard is done."

She barely recognized his voice. "Lord Echo?"

"Helena? I am here." Disoriented, Helen peered from the behemoth's rigor mortis clutch. But all was dark. She smelled a familiar scent, a close derivative to that of Echo's signature. A hybrid was scrutinizing her. She felt its breath. The voice sounded like Echo. But if it was Echo, why would he not be helping to free her?

She extended her right forearm enough to touch the face of her voyeur. More supple than Echo's face. Cold and smooth like the surface of a pond in Spring. Three extra lumps were between his eyes. He had molted. Helen's marks would no longer be on him, but would remain on his evacuated skin. Their ethereal ties had been severed. Their communion was broken.

It spoke, "I must make this fast. You belong here... and I do not. I go now."

"Lord, don't...," Helena struggled desperately. "Your body is vulnerable. I must check you."

Her movement startled Ruhyn. "Stop kicking me! What is going on?"

Helen pleaded, "You are entranced...Echo, come back!"

An antenna pushed her against the beast. Servandum coerced the centimani arms to grasp tighter. "I changed without your aid...or Bryhan's."

"Where is Bran?"

"Guard Bryhan is truly dead."

Ruhyn spat in disgust, "You killed 'r Clanlord?"

Helena bit her lip to contain her muddled anger, which seemed to form a toxic cloud around her. Indeed, mucus clogged her nostrils. Her brow moistened. "Please, don't leave me alone...you need me!"

"You don't need him. I'll get you out of this." Ruhyn shifted frantically, to no avail. Resigned to their confinement, his ghostly spirit and that of her pelt nestled together in the ether. They studied Servandum with trepidation.

You are not alone. Servandum acknowledged the stares of two feline auras, both as brilliant green as of burning copper. *You were tasked to protect me, and you did. As I have changed, so must you.*

"Lord Echo—"

"I am not Echo." This quieted her. Servandum's right antenna curled toward his neck, scraped the seeping punctures, and collected drops of the ichor freshly tasted by Veneda. Then he brushed six radiating rays about Helen's empty left eye socket: the Empress's sigil. "Let our sign help you *see* your own purpose. Serve yourself." Helena heard him, but did not comprehend his words. He had spoken in an archaic elder speech that Doctor Grave occasionally used. Servandum was unaware that he had intuitively switched languages. She looked where his voice trailed, unable to actually see him withdraw.

"Is he gone?" Ruhyn scoffed. "I am almost free. I will fix this…"

Servandum heard him. If the humans got free, they would complicate his departure. There was no need to hurt them, only delay. With a wave of his hands, their minds were spellbound. They would shake the delirium soon enough, but by then he would be gone. He left to join Veneda's side.

The Empress spoke, "Our exit requires a passage. This creature must be further sacrificed. Land will become flesh with its blood, and the artery it creates will deliver us."

"Where is your army? Your colony?"

"We leave without them. They belonged to my previous mate, and their value ended when he perished. I had only maintained order over the brood to find you. A scarcity of suitable mates drove me far and away. Now I return to start anew, Servandum."

The behemoth lay before her, spent of energy. Its rapid flight under earth had exhausted it. It was not designed to have a sustained life. The carcass comprised dozens upon dozens of red-blooded Spawnen; its crimson soul was accordingly incongruous. There was hidden energy within the dead mass. Inside were homunculi. Incorporated into the body during its creation, the mysterious seeds incubated in the warm blood of their Spawnen cousins. As a single homunculus pumped blood within Doctor Grave's chest, a gross of homunculi seeds collectively powered the behemoth.

Veneda summoned them. Her graceful antenna brushed the behemoth, tracing archaic glyphs to amplify her spell. Subtle vibrations coursed from skin to organ. She pressed her head against the behemoth. Then she spoke to the seeds inside, "Burrow home now. To the Ill Orchard from whence all Spawnen come."

In moments, the homunculi answered the summons, compelled to explore the subterranean depths and carve a path to the Orchard they knew as home. First they had to break free from the body in which they were encapsulated. The behemoth's anterior split as pressure mounted from inside. Gouts of blood fountained forth, emptying down and eastward. Spilled entrails lubricated a larger column of coagulum. Surfing the gore was the homunculi seeds. Blood coursed toward the hybrids' feet, surging as the hole in the centimani widened. The ground repelled the liquid at first. It balled up like quicksilver, rolling atop the earth into the mineshaft.

Servandum had never seen these types of homunculi before. He had seen Doctor Grave's heart, and the empty husks in the once-Queen's Hollow. All those had been humanoid shaped. These were eldritch monstrosities including crippled spiders, polydactyl griffins, and dipygus birds. Deformed mutants struggled to remove their wings out of the gore, crawling like crabs.

Veneda, sorceress of flesh and earth, explained to her confused mate, "That was not as natural a birth as if they had matured on the stems of the Ill Trees. But the gut of the many-bodied behemoth proved a sufficient womb."

Bloody rivulets hardened as they flowed. The blood's glow dimmed as the Land took its power. The limestone floors began to suffuse with internal light, first becoming living flesh, then cold meat as it grayed. The mineshaft illumed like a candle then, as if the stone was mere beeswax marbled with black arteries, diffused light lit the once-stone. The earth shifted and trembled as it transformed. The weight of miles of mountainous stone now compressed upon a softening base. Thousands of minor passages collapsed. Fractures and faults split the Land.

"The walls cannot sustain themselves. They will fold into rotten heaps behind us," Veneda explained as she took Servandum's hand in hers and led him into the living corridor. "Hurry now. Follow me."

The royal hybrids left by fantastical means to the Ill Orchard. They descended into the center of the earth in a transient gall, the many pathways they opened in the earth simultaneously inviting vampyric wyverns to come to the Hearth. The Underworld serpents encroached the centimani that wrapped the vulnerable Land dwellers, and began to devour it…

RUHYN AWOKE TO the sounds of slithering wyverns. He made to get away but could not move. Suddenly, the smell of putrid meat assailed him. His stomach heaved. Convulsing for a time, his body eventually relaxed. Then another scent undercut the pall, that of ash and moist limestone. The refreshing smells of earth diffused into his nose. He was indeed home, in Tonn Tomb. Cave dust and humidity embraced him welcomingly, as would his long lost family. But his family was not here and his homeland was infested with carnivorous serpents.

The sucking, rattling, and gorging amplified.

His neck was throbbing. Turning his head would have alleviated the pain. The behemoth still held tight, but now its resistance was not that of the elastic living; rigor mortis had petrified its countless appendages. The monstrosity must have died whilst clutching him…and one other. Beneath him in death's embrace was a warm victim. A weak heartbeat pulsed against his helmet, under his right ear. Memories flooded his mind.

"Helen?" He squirmed.

"Ruhyn?" Her chapped lips spoke softly. "Can… you… move?"

"Yes. I may have a way out, I think."

She pleaded. "I need…water."

Wyverns continued to shuffle and slurp. Ruhyn wondered how long the white serpents had been nibbling away. How many were there? How long ago had they been asleep? "I'll fetch some," he promised. "After I get the serpents away."

As Ruhyn wiggled downward, he constantly turned. Rotating was the easiest way to progress. Teeth from compressed alien faces tore at his clothes. Talons raked his chest. Dead, brittle fingers broke awkwardly, until his hindquarters jutted free. Leveraging against his blowpipe, he pushed himself out from the carcass's embrace.

As he stood upright, the slurping ceased as if the darkness noted his presence. Uneasiness flowed through the shadows, soaking into Ruhyn. Chills ran through his nerves, streaming out of his neck hairs. His ruckus had caused attention. The sound of scaled bellies brushing stone signaled doom. Darts would not penetrate their natural armor. Blunt strikes from the iron shaft may work, but slowly. He was outnumbered. He needed to see. He needed a better weapon: fire. The Tomb's funerary pyre, if stirred to life, could repel the wyverns. Illuminating the chamber would also allow him to see."

"I will be back soon enough. You may be safer behind all these limbs than roaming free. Do not stray without me."

"I can't move…," Helen rasped.

Ruhyn dropped to the cavern's floor. Scrabbling about, he assayed its slope and texture. His left hand felt sand. Frantically, he crawled, patting the ground. More sand, but now it was a softer, ash-laden mixture. This unique powder surrounded the ceremonial bier at the cavern's center. The monument's glass effigies rested higher than the surrounding to allow rainwater to flow away. Monoliths of glass stood atop like trees. Numerous pots were filled with colored salts; flintstone could be found beside any of the cauldron-like fonts.

He crawled upward. His hands found a sharp edge of hewn stone, the perimeter of the Hearth. Adrenaline accelerated his heartbeat. Ruhyn stooped as he reached out with his stave: tapping, prodding, and sweeping. He hoped to connect with some font or angled sarcophagus to orient himself. His feet and pipe had explored beneath a tilting crystal, found nothing, inviting him to advance and crash his helmet with glass. Crack! Neither helmet or glass broke. The impact excited the wyverns, but they fed too well on blood to investigate.

Ruhyn felt the polished tincal-glass shaft with his hands, determining its dimension from its angles and widths. He recognized the owner from its shape. "Oh, Lady Sahra Tonn. You're rescue'n me from despair." He pressed his helm's brow against the sculpture. He remembered her death stance. Her white bodice stretched above her shoulders like angel wings, held by her joined hands. Lengthy, flat gray hair and hazel eyes stared at him. He could feel her emotions of pride and hope. A tear of joy dripped down his cheek. He knew exactly where he stood within the Hearth now. Lady Sahra had birthed two metalworkers, the elder was Brownsmith Huiln and the junior Blacksmith Grovel. Grovel had been mysteriously taken in the Ill Age and was not honored under earth yet, but Son Huiln died years prior the cataclysm and was rightly encased beside his mother. Adjacent to Huiln's copper laden body was his font to make green fire, a steel pot full of cuprous salt and ingots.

Ruhyn advanced cautiously forward. His left hand braced his pipe, and his right reached forward to touch what would should be the font...

Unexpectedly, his hand found an out of place form. His fingers investigated. Smooth, lamellar plates. Serpentine scales!

He pulled away, tumbling backwards. Bracing for a wyvern's attack, he lowered his pipe as if it were a pike.

Nothingness pressed over him.

In the background, the gnashing of wyvern continued unabated.

He made for the cauldron again. He poked the area where the scaled-thing had been. It was still there. It too had a pole. It was completely inanimate. Lowering his weapon, Ruhyn felt it. Its torso was indeed scaled. Instinct pulled him a step back. This time he did not cower low to the earth. Instead he held his ground set into a defensive posture. Part of him understood that the wyverns did not take human form, so the man must have been armored somehow.

"Clanlord Bryhan? Your Gray Lord has indeed abandoned you. Too much is happen' here, forgive me now as I leave to ignite the font." Ruhyn struck flint. Sparks caught the tinder in the bowl. The minerals burned ghostly green, though puffs of pastel blue raised from intermixed zinc powder. The columnar sarcophagi refracted this splendor, and brightened Son Bryhan who stood ready to join his encased family. "I will put you to rest properly, my Lord. I do promise you that honor. That may be another day, for now I must deal with vermin." As brilliant as the flames were, they scarcely lit the chamber. He surveyed the place and spotted Echo's empty shell atop the behemoth's carcass. "Your master looks very dead, Son Bryhan. I will leave you here for a time 'til I save Helen and Burden, if he is out there."

He saw the shadows quiver. There were too many

creatures to count. Better to find an escape route. Three historic passageways were carved into the Tonn Tomb chamber: the archway to the Land's surface was blocked with collapsed boulders; the threshold to the common folk's catacombs was congested with debris; the gateway to mines was now on the opposite side of a newly formed, wyvern-spawning chasm.

The wyverns were attracted to the giant carcass, but they also sought the cancerous, fleshy rock created by the Empress's geomancy. Hundreds of pink eyes and white scales shimmered from the shadow's edge. Years ago, Burden and he had combated one; that had been a dire day. Now, over fifty wyverns gnawed on the behemoth. The centimani itself had created a new entrance into the chamber, but it had closed as quickly as it had opened. The stone nearby blistered like cooling lava, oozing earthly puss; the flesh-stone folded as easily as boneless meat.

Ruhyn's eyes trailed the smoke as it lifted from the font. Vents had been bored to the surface through the white stalactites. The holes were no longer visible, but the smoke dissipated toward that direction, so it must have been porous to air. Unless he grew wings, it was not accessible.

They were trapped.

A bloated leech slithered a few lengths from Helen. It was seven feet long, but only an arm's width thick throughout. Tiny feet pushed it along, unable to support its belly. Its spine bent as it probed its food.

Ruhyn gathered as many torches and firewood as he could. He ignited them in the font, then placed them deliberately around Helen. A fiery wall separated the curer from the nearest threat.

She stirred as the fire warmed her. "Ruhyn!"

"Yes, I am here. And water is coming." Away from the behemoth and wyvern, he identified wet rock. It came from dripping rainwater, which led to a puddle. He gathered some in in his cupped hands. Constrained, she drank awkwardly. Ruhyn could see her now in the shimmering light. Her bandages were missing. The battle and journey had exposed her swollen wounds. A strange tattoo radiated about her left eye. Her lids remained closed as her lips instinctively accepted the water. After two more handfuls, Ruhyn was anxious to move along.

"Time to get you out. Twist your feet. That's it. Now wriggle downward. You'll work your way out the path I had." Ruhyn moved limbs out of her way as she contorted free. Attempting to stand triumphantly, she wearily succumbed to gravity.

She sat, rubbing her eyes. "My head is spinning. Every time I try to focus, my whole head throbs."

Ruhyn comforted her, "Shut them for a moment. The ring of fire will keep you safe from them white crawlers. I aim to locate Burden. That is if this beast took him too. I suppose its grabby hands took all of us from the Keep."

He grabbed a torch and started to search. Burden was nowhere to be seen. He could have been under the beast, smothered. Perhaps he was never taken, his body staying in the Chromlechon. Or, he could be near the anterior of the beast, where the wyvern aggregated. Faint torchlight made it difficult to investigate, for every illuminated crevice cast a strong shadow. So dense was the tangle of limbs, Ruhyn could not see through it.

On the other hand, the light made it easier for Burden to see his Master. "Ruhyn," he wheezed. Ruhyn spotted the ram horn of his friend's helmet protruding just ten yards away near two wyverns. Burden was alive, but in peril. A leech sucked on the arms holding him. It would not be long until it ate its way through.

Advancing torch in one hand, stave in the other, Ruhyn met the gorging serpent and struck. It turned fast, coiling its base and lower feet, the front two-thirds stood erect. Swaying in the air, it lashed its forked tongue. It turned its head right and left. Then it lunged. Ruhyn parried, dropping his torch to hold his pipe with both hands. The serpent arched again. Its mouth spat a warning.

Flaring blazes twirled about Helen as she entered the fray, a torch in either hand, blindly carving out a sphere of smoke.

Ruhyn darted out of her way. He dodged and yelled, "I am not a serpent!" He yelled. "Can you see what you're doin'?"

"Well enough to find you. I can hear better."

"Aim away from my voice. To your right, now!"

The wyvern backed into the shadows away from her. It disappeared. Seconds later, it emerged erect, poised atop a stalagmite. The white snake lunged upon Ruhyn. He held his pipe with both hands over his head, horizontal. Diverted, the wyvern spiraled about the shaft. Too heavy and too danger-ous keep aloft, he dropped it. Before the scaled leech could unravel itself, he stepped onto both ends of it. So leveraged, the writhing snake was compressed onto the ground, coughing up recently imbibed blood. Maintaining pressure, Ruhyn bounded up and down. The frequent pulses did little to the leech other than provoke anger.

"Come here with the fire."

Helen approached.

Ruhyn fought to maintain his balance. "Feed it."

Helen arrived, inserting the brand into the open maw. The fire was engulfed in the throat. Ruhyn continued pressing it into the ground while Helen lodged the brand deeper. The serpent choked. Its head glowed like a lantern. Ash and ember spat with steaming blood. Eventually, the eaten torch dimmed as the creature's movements slowed.

Ruhyn squatted over the struggling enemy. It was immobilized if not dead. They needed to finish it off. Leaving the wyvern occupied momentarily, he scampered, looking for a large rock. He grabbed a slab, and released it over the thing's head.

Wielding his pipe again, Ruhyn called to Helen to light the area around Burden.

"Are you ready to be freed?" Ruhyn asked.

Unsteady light splashed on the man's helmet. Burden gasped for air.

"Aye, friend. I am hurrin'." Ruhyn wriggled the end of his stave under the wing that compressed his companion's helmet. The horned ram-head was revealed. It turned. Ruhyn saw his friend's arms were bound and could not remove the mask. Supporting the iron bar on his shoulder, Ruhyn managed to keep the behemoth's wing extended while freeing Burden's right hand. With that, he maneuvered the helmet until it came free. Burden breathed deep, gasping for air.

Meanwhile Helen swatted with fire. She saw many blurred white entities. She perceived them all to be serpents. Her heart raced. Every pulse shook her vision. She coughed, then struck the air proactively. Once she sensed the presence of the white Empress skulking. The vision dissipated with a swipe of fire. Thrice she attacked earthen formations thinking they were serpentine. She fell to her knees frequently out of breath. Empresses? Wyverns perching atop stalagmites? What was real? Fantasy?

Meanwhile, Ruhyn continued to pry petrified limbs until Burden was free. They collapsed to their knees exhausted. Helen was walking in a protective circle, striking the air with flaming brands. Staring through countless silhouettes of stalagmites against the backlight of the green brazier, the three began to assess their peril.

Ruhyn summarized, "Serpents keep coming, Burden. All of the exits 'r blocked now. There's no retreatin' to the mines because the ground opened up. Wyverns keep crawling from it. They're attracted to that heap of blood 'n flesh." The behemoth's anterior had been sucked dry, and still the wyverns dripped from atop in a knotted mass; they began to feed on one another like an infestation of maggots. "We must retreat to the Hearth. And we must go now."

Burden donned his helmet, his biceps swollen and

sweaty. He nodded to confirm his readiness. A weary Helen passed her torches to Ruhyn, then leaned into him, draping her arm over his shoulder for support. They scrambled toward the ceremonial Hearth.

Suddenly, Burden hesitated. He held out hand to stop Ruhyn. "Back."

"Where? Why? We need to light the grand fire. Come, now—"

"Sunny."

Ruhyn stared with disbelief into his friend's eyes. How does one negotiate with the delirious? "We haven't time for your mind to go sour on us. Come now. Head to the Hearth. We must ignite it, else we have nowhere to go but into their bellies!"

Burden was not coherent enough to obey. He turned around frantically. Listening. Looking. Then he ran into the shadows.

"Burden, no!" Ruhyn swore. He looked toward the bier. A wyvern plopped from the top of Lady Sahra's pillar. The creatures would overrun the place if the fires were not lit soon. "Curses. Helen and I are movin' forward."

Ruhyn headed toward the glass monuments where he sat Helen next to Son Bryhan's feet. He lit a dozen more braziers, each fueled by a different mineral and burning a different hue. A myriad of colors diffused through the glass tombs on into the chamber.

He watched the wyverns with horror. They fed on the behemoth, themselves, and the once-stone. As long as there was fuel by the Hearth, they could shield themselves with fire. But to what end? The ceremonial pyre was designed to be viewed from outside its perimeter, though tile pathways did network across the flammable floor. The cauldron fonts rested atop its extended bed of wooden tinder. It could not burn hot enough to melt the tincal-glass, so when it lit, the columnar tombs appeared to be crystals growing from a bed of fire. Ruhyn was prepared to light portions of the Hearth soon. He had to keep the leeches away. When lit, there would be a barrier between them and the underworld serpents. He wanted Burden back, but Ruhyn dared not venture out now to find him.

Ruhyn proceeded by lighting the northern beds. He decided to ignite only those he must, to minimize the use of fuel and to prolong their stand. The fire leapt across the tile ways on its own accord, so the eastern section flared spontaneously. The conflagration pushed the leeches further away, and the roar of the flames drowned the sounds of their eating. Great plumes drew upward through the invisible vents in the ceiling.

A smoking, horned body crept into view. It collapsed beside Bryhan's feet.

"Burden, you're back!"

"No Sun." Burden sat in the smoke. Allowed it to wash over him.

"The smoke is good. We survive for now, friend. I admit to not knowin' how we're getting' out of this. I won't be dying in the gut of a snake. If we die here, we will die in this fire."

Ruhyn's last captain assented. "Die clean."

"I do not want to die. But I am getting dizzy…" Helen's

head nodded under newfound weight. Bathed in smoke, the two men joined her, likewise submitting to oxygen deprivation…

LYSIS HAD GONE immediately to the Underworld, searching for Echo and his party. He saw the devastation the behemoth brought to the once-Queen's Hollow. He took long note of the outlandish, rotting lapisplasm formations. He tracked the congested arteries away from the Keep. His sword breached clogs of once-stone, but it continuously buckled upon itself. Several times the flesh collapsed about him. It was tedious to excavate himself and lost a day's time before returning to the surface.

Meanwhile, the Doctor had cleared the bogs and surrounding fields of living or infectious dangers, during which time he managed to collect specimens for study: hybrid skeletons, homunculi, and blood of all types. Only two hundred hybrids were estimated to have wandered into the wild. Grave was sure that many of those were wounded. Besides, all were sterile. There was no threat of them reproducing or infiltrating the Keep.

Lysis collected Grave to hunt atop the Land. The behemoth's general trajectory had been toward the East, to Tonn City. Lysis and his retinue gathered in its ruined city center, the Commons Amphitheater. The undead Lord guised himself and his partners with a spell. The urchins and homeless would not see the retinue for what it was. The truth would have scared them. Instead, the Tonn folk would see their long missing Clanlord Kaiyn. The curators appeared as if they were the Lord Kaiyn's missing Legion; their magical pennants bore the Clanlord's sigil, two rampant wyverns addorsed. The eldritch ant mounts assumed the appearance of horses. Doctor Grave, the demonic butcher truly responsible for Tonn's calamity and the Legion's demise, took the appearance of Apothecary Whitebeard, Kaiyn's physician.

Lysis stood in the center of the fire atop slabs of stones. Resistant to heat, he performed a rite he had done many times before. Balling his hands into fists, he flexed until a surfeit of white ichor bled. Speaking words in the ancient, eldritch tongue, *lapis elixir* dripped into the flames, and energy exchanged between the corporeal and ethereal. Painful memories of his lost children were consumed with each burning drop. Angelic effigies of his sons and daughters puffed from each aliquot of his molten blood, connecting its potential energy to his. A satellite Pyre was thus prepared.

His regiment of curers circled about the fire. They sacrificed art to feed their Lord. Pennants snapped in the pulsing wind. Draughts ushered his paper minions from their roosting. Embers flared with each gust of air, only to wane in their absence. Smoke rose continuously from the ground. He had explored every lead on that range in vain. The Empress had planned her escape route well. She understood the means that her pursuers would employ to follow, and left a confusing trail.

Doctor Grave spoke, "She played us at the Keep. And again, as she fled. She laid false trails faster than we could investigate them. Her behemoth's trail ran east, as did the Empress's. Yet there are over a hundred passageways of lapisplasm in the Calx, all sealed and impassable. We know not where she went from here. The Empress's path runs cold."

"We need help from Clan Tonn."

"Few remain," the Doctor replied. "Do you really think they can see things we cannot?"

Lysis did not entertain Grave's conversation. The surviving population knew their Land well, and he needed their perspective. The Lord entered the variegated fire to summon them. His curators continued to feed it while it birthed sprites. *Ferrus Eviscamir* rested in his hands, reflecting the moonlight as he waited for the minions to bring a human with a promising aura. Outwardly, he appeared patient and still. Internally, his soul was burning with anger. His desire to act, his frustration in not knowing where to go, enraged him. Higher and higher his white fire swelled. His ashen minions were sent. In hours, a group of orphans gathered, following the sprites.

The elderly came too. A crone crawled atop overturned stone, covered in soot, following eleven glowing sprites. Her soul was weighted down with years of madness. Images of Grave haunted her. She had escaped his reaping of women years ago by hiding in the mountains. She was a mature woman then, and that was twenty years ago. During the Ill Age. Now, older yet and accustomed to despair, she was enticed by magical folds of paper. She looked at Grave with recognition and smiled. Her soul was fooled.

"Me word. Aiyn, weeturned!" She mumbled, eyes wide.

"Word. Wear word!"

The curers ascended the stone to offer aid.

"Womb oh 'ire!" She yammered with her toothless grin. Caring hands raised to her feet. "Womb. Oh phwire."

Lysis struggled to interpret her words, twisted by her own mouth. Faint memories of ceremonies took form from her words: colored fire, glass pillars, and burial rites. Her boney fingers pointed toward the East, seventy yards whence she had come. A tower had fallen there. Smoke billowed from under it. "Word. Wee you the 'earth smoke? Womb. Be phired!"

"My Lady. What do you say through your broken mouth?"

Her soul spoke clearly: *"Clanlord Kaiyn, your Legion has returned!"* To the elderly women with raspberry eyes, sunken cheeks, mangy grime-incrusted hair, Lord Lysis did not confirm or deny her hallucinations.

"My Lord," spoke the crone's spirit. *"Don't you remember? The kilns of the city use charcoal. Not wood. Pine smells sour. Oak bitter. I smell more back there. Smoke from our City's Hearth. Tonn Tomb. It has not been lit since the Ill Age."*

"What does that mean?"

"Lord," her soul curtsied. *"Funeral biers smells differen' than fire. Someone is havin' a funeral for royalty below groun'."*

He darted toward the fallen athanor indicated. He cut the stoney earth nearby with *Ferrus Eviscamir*. Then he worked with ferocity until his blade penetrated the cavern's ceiling. He dove into the dark well, smoke enveloping his form.

The radiant warlord Kaiyn Tonn shot into the chamber like a solar flare emitted by the royal Hearth. The Lord's illusion held, even confusing Bryhan, who saw his father's spirit descending, surfing on roiling plumes of earth. Between the stone teeth of the cavern's ceiling, the Clanlord rode this torrent on his warhorse, swinging his great flail *Wyvern*, named in honor of the creatures that adorned his blazon. Now the Clanlord returned to clear the subterranean passages under his namesakes' city once again.

"Father Kaiyn, did you not die in my embrace? Blind and crazed by Echo's uncontrolled feeding?" Bryhan was not alone in his wonder. Aleece and the dormant souls of royal Tonn reminisced about their mobility and greatness.

Behind Clanlord Kaiyn, atop a following wave of debris infused with celestial radiance, came the thundering charge of his mounted Legion: dozens of warriors, lances lowered, and pennons waving. The horses rode on the air, breaching the cavern, and tracked the interior of the cave as they descended. A river of fresh air lapped their rapid descent. The oxygenated air infused the royal bier. Towering flames swelled. Shadows shrank from the roaring conflagration. Bolts of heat shot like meteors as if the sun had just collapsed into earth's embrace. A swarming tangle of ivory serpents awaited to cushion his fall. Kaiyn moved faster than the ether could move. Sparkling effigies traced his violent path. *Wyvern* slashed, whipped, and cut. Scales impermeable to regular steel, gave way. Pulsating afterglows of his silhouette lingered as he meted out death. Closer, Whitebeard led another attack.

Then, for Son Bryhan anyway, the spell dissipated. He grew worried as he witnessed Doctor Grave join Lysis and his retinue. Bryhan stole a look at the living and dead. How would they perceive the necromancer? Lord Lysis and his party proved skilled in deception. Deceased Ladies and Lords misinterpreted Doctor Grave as Apothecary Whitebeard. Ruhyn, Helen, and Burden, exhausted and overwhelmed, no longer knew the difference between reality and fantasy, were woozy, and slipped seamlessly from awareness into dream.

"Whitebeard! Here!" Bryhan's shade called telepathically, going along with the play. *"You must save them."*

Grave as the old apothecary navigated the flaming vats. In an instant, Helen and Ruhyn were over his shoulders. He was off immediately to a cool recess, muttering commands to the Legion. Lysis' curators stormed the Hearth and retrieved the unconscious Burden and the dead Bryhan before fire swept over them.

Lord Lysis relentlessly fought the wyverns off, *Ferrus Eviscamir* cutting magically through their enameled skin. White blood and red sluiced off his magical blade, separating into two streams, as would oil and water. Many serpents were cut down. Yet more came, their ranks replenishing from the chasm from which the Empress had left. Blood attracted them, even blood of their own kin. His sword blazing hot, Lysis dismounted the once-Queen and prepared to seal the crag. He cut stalagmites at their base and sliced the newly formed lapisplasm formations. The ground quaked. Blood wept unnaturally from the terrain. The chasm was clotted with flesh and soil. The parasites' advance ceased abruptly.

Victorious, Grave and Lysis gathered about Bryhan and the humans, leaving Echo's empty casing to lay eerily apart.

"Lord, the Empress came here for him," Bryhan's soul spoke, *"She left through the crag from which the serpents came."*

Grave assessed, *"Lord, They came under the pretense of waging war. But she did not want our land. Nor our lives. She only wanted Echo. She even abandoned her colony for him."*

"Tell me about the Foundling." Lysis demanded.

"Lord Lysis, Echo is not himself. His bestial instinct usurped his humanity. He molted into his final state ...he left with the Empress voluntarily. He renounced his name. She renamed him Servandum."

The once-Queen began speaking cryptically in ancient tongues. Grave translated for the others, *"Man has dressed in the bones of the elders. We elders have consumed humans. Always, we Spawnen conspire to remix our bloodlines. Such carnal desires drove our disease. A he-wasp and she-bird united, birthing a chromantaur. The Foundling."*

"We must follow Echo," Lysis approached the sealed crag.

"I advise against it." Grave replied, to which Lysis tightened his sword grip. *"It would be dangerous, my Lord."* Stepping back and hiding his ax from view. *"We have never experienced her type of sorcery. Her cunning has already led us astray. This chasm appears to have one entrance. But as the behemoth's route branched, we can assume this one has multiple*

exits. Any pathway they traveled is likely to be a dynamic artery. One that roots and moves through earth, changing its position. We could be trapped as you were before."

The once-Queen began communicating again. Lysis understood fragments but glared at Grave to translate again. *"My Queen says that Empress goes back to her homeland."* The Doctor listened again, *"A homeland that also once belonged to her ancestors, who were exiled hundreds of years ago."*

The earth rumbled. *"Her tunnels shift beneath us,"* declared Grave.

"Explain," Lysis said.

The golem continued, *"The elder ants' origin lies beyond the Underworld. The same place the Empress came from, though it is remote and unknown to us. We will need to track them through the earth with someone who is still connected to the chromantaur formerly known as Echo."*

All turned toward Helen. Her left eye sourced a brilliant ring of six lashing, tongues of fire: the Empress's sigil.

"We'll take Helen." Lysis affirmed. "Her vision requires healing. Wake the glassmaker. We require his skill. I'll prepare a pyre." He walked into the Hearth, slitting his hand with *Eviscamir*. He squeezed his *lapis elixir* into the fire.

A whirlwind erupted, pulling the flock of paper sprites down from the Commons above. The company of curators immediately began immolating offerings. Their skeletal Lord kneeled and lifted Helen up, and returned to the blaze. She was laid onto a glass sarcophagus which now served as an altar.

Doctor Grave set to work. Crystals of sal ammoniac

jolted Ruhyn awake. He moaned, slowly regaining his senses. He looked about for Helen. He spotted her silhouette on the glass dais. Then he saw Apothecary Whitebeard kneeling mere inches away.

"The Lord has a task for you."

Refocusing on the long lost physician, Ruhyn gradually realized it was actually Doctor Grave.

"Master Ruhyn, Lord Lysis needs you to craft Helen a glass eye. As you promised her."

"How'd you know what I had pledged?"

"I read your mind. He'll need that to restore…amplify rather… her vision."

Have you no bounds? Ruhyn was speechless for a moment. "It'd just be for show. Do you intend to possess her?" His mind conjured a terrible image, with Helen's corpse being resurrected. "Is she…?" Ruhyn tried to stand.

The masked physician waved his hand, leaned forward, and spoke softly, "Calm yourself. She is as she was before you sought refuge in the hearth. If you understood the Rules of Animation, you would know that even if Lysis reanimates her left eye, her soul and heart will remain her own. Sight of a new kind will develop. By having you craft her eye, as per the Rule of Relics—"

"I don't need to know all y'r rules. But I will do it, if it helps her."

Grave handed Ruhyn his blowpipe.

Ruhyn scoffed, "A finer pipe and lampwork are needed for this, not that. I won't be usin' that. You don't need to know these details, do ya? Like I don't need to know y'r rules."

"You must know that we intend to use it as a vessel," Grave halted him, "You must prepare the shell. Lord Lysis will treat her eye and place it inside. You must close it. Upon completion, we will implant it by special means."

"The heat will burn whatever you put within it."

"We will ensure that the eyepiece, its filling, and its host are not harmed."

Ruhyn shook his head to brush off the alchemy he did not understand. He retrieved the pouch and gave it to the Doctor. No longer beset by wyverns, he cleared debris from around the burning furnace. Then he scoured the chamber for glass ingots.

Lord Lysis filled a metal bowl with his ichor. Grave placed the desiccated eyeball into this. The flesh rehydrated. Lysis' retinue fed the Pyre with offerings, which infused the souls in the Hearth with newfound energy. They excitedly applauded Ruhyn, offering him unsolicited advice as he prepared a workstation.

Ruhyn fashioned glass shells, each decorated with a blue disc to match her right iris's azure. With care, he introduced slight asymmetry with thin red filaments. Ruhyn reported, "Lord and Doctor, I am ready. Tongs, flames, and canes of soft glass, I have, 'n molds of imperial porphyry. I practiced my recipe on surrogate stones. Three small globes are prepared, though only one is needed. I am ready for her eye."

The bowl with Helen's eye was delivered to Ruhyn. The buoyant sphere rotated in the bowl as if it swam. He collected it with forceps, placed it inside a shell's open side. Liquid sizzled as it coated the interior. After the temperature equilibrated and smoke ceased, he gathered a cane, melted it atop the opening, and sealed the hole.

Ruhyn rotated the eye in a cooler part of the flame with his tools. The sphere smoothed. "A few hours more, Lord. The glass needs to cool slowly, lest it crack."

"Give me the eye," Lysis instructed. "My sorcery will temper it."

"Still, it will burn her…"

Lysis took the glowing hot eye in his hand. "My blood will protect her." Into the fire he went. Lord Lysis drew forth *Eviscamir*. He slit open his wrist and emptied *lapis elixir* into her socket. Electricity arced. The Doctor approached the altar, blocking Ruhyn's line of sight.

Suddenly Helen's back arched. Lysis cradled her and walked out of the hearth. His retinue, albeit a loyal crew, took a step back. They may have harbored some jealousy and wonder toward the woman who received their sacrifices and their Lord's attention. They did not recognize her yet as a woman from their own Keep. To them, Helen was an Outsider turned Seer.

The Lord presented Helen to the glassworker: her left eye had no lid, the right was closed. "Hold her until she comes to."

HELEN DREAMED. SHE straddled Echo's bare thorax. His entire body was brilliant white, and felt more solid than ever before. He was giving her a tour of a world utterly unfamiliar. He moved so fast that the wind blew her hair aloft; it fluttered like a flag. The journey took her through an ossified landscape where gangly tree trunks were made of cytoplasm wrapped with lamellar shells of bone and leafed with sloughs of veined skins. The ground beneath them was corporeal tissue, in parts calloused or scabbed with mountainous cruor. Echo charged through this and into a swamp of molten blood. Above them, clouds mirrored the hue of rosy seas below them. Red rain fell in obscure curtains.

The bleeding Sky doused an Ill Orchard in the distance, which they soon traversed. The trunks therein were grotesque unions of hybrids. Sculpted or turned to stone whilst copulating. Twisted stems grew from these. There the fruit was crowned with flower-mantled embryos. Some fell to the ground. Crows picked at these, revealing the pithy contents: golem seeds. Homunculi shaped as miniature Spawnen: rocs, insects, and humans. Fertilized, the fruit ripened into winged eldritch things. Sickly children roamed this ill place, bewildered humanoid dryads with green tinged skin. With them, eldritch ants crawled and featherless rocs squealed. They were harvested by the chromanti. The hybrids collected the living fruit, weakened the Spawnen by draining them of color and wheeled them away in cages of bone.

Unencumbered, Echo advanced faster than the vehicles, and Helen had to hold tight so as not to fall. He did not run away from them as she expected. The wagons of the enslaved lined up behind him. He was leading them down a highway lined with ivory obelisks. At the end was a ziggurat made of flesh, stepped in lapisplasm. A bridge lifted them over a moat of mucus. In a flash, they had arrived at their destination.

He stopped, letting her dismount and turned.

Then she saw his face. It was not Echo's. There were too many eyes.

"Who are you?" She muttered in horror.

He mouthed his new name: "Servandum."

Invisible frost needled her neck. Soft hair hardened to icicles. Blood from the humid air condensed on her forehead. She paled. Was he leaching her soul?

Panicking she turned, looking over her shoulder looking for a way out. There was no escape.

Servandum still stared intensely. His eyes focused beyond Helen at another. The Empress materialized beside her. The hybrids interlocked their arms and looked in unison at Helen. Her body burned doubly with frostbite. Her blood congealed in her veins. Her skin turned paler, to gray. They fed on her body's color, stealing her essence.

"Noooo!" Helen fell to her knees...

She awoke shivering in Ruhyn's warm embrace. Helen stammered, "I saw something posing as Echo, but the imposter had extra eyes." She had spoken before she realized where she was, or knew who was with her. "Ruhyn, you are alive." Then memory rushed into her mind. She remembered being blind. "I can see!"

Her healing right eye saw the world as it had before: a colorful world, the spirit world invisible. Her left eye saw it as the undead *see:* a gray world, with colored spirits. Her brain attempted to reconcile these as she examined Ruhyn. Helen thought to herself, *I see your green lion soul. Your body is gray. I see my prairie cat's ghost snuggled against it. Both vibrant. Translucent. I see ghosts? Do I still dream?*

Grave came quickly, "You do not dream now, nor did you dream. You *saw*. Speak more."

"I know not the boundary between my dreams and reality. I rode upon my master's back in a hellish world."

"Echo is alive?" the Doctor asked.

Helen answered, "I saw Echo in the vision, but he called himself Servandum." *But where is his loyal Guard now? Oh, there. Amongst the beautiful array of sarcophagi.* She quieted as she assessed the situation: Echo has left us, and his blood has left you. *You are truly dead, Bran. But I can see your soul! And your ancestors!*

The others were anxious for her to speak. They circled about her, prompting her to continue: "I saw trees ripe with fruit shaped like humans and creatures, being harvested and put into cages." She told of the Ill Orchard, and the Land of Flesh. People in peril. This brought the attention of Lord Lysis, who filtered through the group of curators to her side.

And then she saw the Lord. *Saw* his soul.

Helen gasped.

His death's head was enflamed; sparks of lightning crowned his aura; his confidence filled every footstep, each depression overfilling with his power like fiery coals; his majesty like the sun and radiance like a full moon. His soul extended into the cosmos: tendrils of connected stars. A necklace of hate fueled him: the ghosts of his four brothers. A wreath of divine locks chained his soul to his body: his children's hair. He had been more attached to this Land than his detached disposition let on. *Where is the soul of his wife?*

"Lady Maeve has been lost to the bogs," Lysis replied telepathically. *"I did not send her there."*

She heard him mindspeak. She thought, *Perhaps I am possessed like Bryhan had been.* "Am I dead?"

"Your left eye is. I restored sight to it so you can assist me in my quest. It sees how the dead see, so the ethereal world is now revealed to you."

"I fear you, Lord."

"You detect the darkness that motivates me."

"Why pay special attention to me? One who is not of your retinue?"

"There are more people to rescue in a hidden, unchartered land. Servandum goes to them. You have astral ties to him. With your connection and sight, you can track his path."

"I am in your debt for healing me, my Lord." *Do you own part of my soul? I am not like your refined curers. I seem incompatible with them. Do you possess me?*

"No one possesses you. Your service to Echo is broken, though bonds linger which we will rely on to guide us. You and I are now connected in some measure, but you are not enslaved to me. I do not control your heart. After this quest, you are free to leave my service."

To the retinue Keepers, Helen was no longer a misfit;

she was even more outlandish now. They questioned her role:

"Who is she?"

"What is she?"

"A sorceress?"

Helen did not belong to any community. Not with the Keepers back in the Chromlechon, nor with the retinue of curators, nor with the Outsiders of Tonn. She was an independent force, joining Lysis on a mission. She was expected to go to the fore, climb atop the once-Queen to ride tandem with the Grey Lord. Her feline aura circled her, reinforcing her courage as she walked through Lysis' curers.

She addressed them, "Call me, Helen."

"Seer Helen," Lord Lysis added, her title providing more authority. "You will serve her as you obey me."

To Ruhyn, Helen was a friend. Knowing that she planned to depart, but not when she may return, he queried, "So you go with Lord Lysis, to rescue Echo?"

Lysis answered, "We go not to for him, but to free the people oppressed in the land he retreats to, Master Ruhyn. I will return with a city's worth of men, women, and children. They will seek sanctuary in the City's halls."

"But I do not own the city. Those that do, the Lords of Tonn, are here. Dead. All but Son Bryhan sealed in clear stone. Who shall you seek permission from, when all the Lords are dead?"

"I know the dead. Their souls speak to me. You have earned your place. Your ancestors count on you to host those we save. They give you the charge of the city. You are the governor of the City and have a lot of work to do to get it restored, Lord Ruhyn."

"Aye, Lord of the Keep, if the royal dead say so," Ruhyn stood in shock. He bowed to the sacred Hearth. "The City will welcome any you save. I will restore Tonn as soon as I am able to climb to the surface, or I am not the Master of Joy."

Helen sensed a measure of anxiety in the reluctant leader of Tonn, one unwilling to call himself Lord. She assured him, "Lord Ruhyn, I will listen for you people's laughter to guide us home."

Lord Lysis addressed the Doctor, "Use *Hewnmaw* to reopen the passageway leading to the Mines and Commons. Remove the downed columns, allow the doors to swing open. Lead Ruhyn and his captain to the surface."

"Lord, I will be quick so I can join you—"

"Grave, you will stay here. Attend to the Keep. Govern it until my return."

"Yes…," he paused trying to keep his dreams of exploring the Ill Orchard from dissipating. He failed. "Of course, Lord."

Lysis commanded, "I will take a score of curers, but the rest will remain here and at the Keep to maintain the Pyres." To his scout he indicated, "Seer Helen, lead the way forward."

Her left eye, graced with Servandum's mark and Lysis' ichor, saw phantoms of the Empress immersed in the jammed fissure. She motioned toward the sealed chasm where the ghosts struggled, half immersed in stone. An obvious choice, but was it the correct one? Could she really see the trail better than he?

"We will require an Underworld crawler." Lysis called to his flock. Each centimani heart that remained intact would be reanimated. To make this happen, his curators rolled up hundreds of drawings, soaking up power in the magical fire. The art pieces imbibed steaming *lapis elixir* before snaking their way toward the behemoth's carcass. White blood was thus funneled from the fire into the dead, half-eaten centimani.

Ruhyn witnessed in horror as the centimani regained its posture, clumsily waddling to the crag. It began to dig in the softened stone, unearthing wyvern carcasses. It was as if the undead behemoth exhumed some demonic mass grave. Yet it was merely opening a gate to a lower world.

Lord, Seer, and a score of curators, lined up behind it. They departed into the flesh tunnel, descending into hell, riding atop once-Queen, burrowing after the Empresses' trail. Into the unknown.

Ruhyn watched in awe as the void closed around them.

Epilogue: Operating Theater Birth

"RISE, MY DAUGHTERS."

Three little girls, bare, cold and filthy, slipped off the table. They shuffled toward the voice and waited in line. Residual clay dripped onto the floor and dried into gritty cake. The Doctor dressed them in blood-stained aprons. Then they sat down in a semi-circle at his feet. The group of four was alone in the Operating Theater.

"There are rules I have never taught the humans, those I call Keepers. I could not teach them before, since I just learned them myself. Geomancy was a lost art, forgotten by my maker and her descendants." He paused to analyze the three spent homunculi husks before him, and smiled at the fourth, ripe with power hydrating in a bowl. "My Queen knew some geomancy, long ago. Enough to create her nurses and curers. Me. She never practiced geomancy since. In fact, she could not, for all the materials required were spent when she started her colony."

The three listened intently. One had a tendency to smile, and did. One was overwhelmed with sensations, and shivered in awe. The last was prone to tear, and wept without knowing why.

The Doctor held his ax *Hewnmaw* before him and re-read the promise inscribed on the handle: *Children, may this blade carve you life.* "When my Queen's colony succumbed to disease, I strived to create my own family from earth with this ax. Creating life was nigh impossible. This tool, and my promise, was not enough. I learned that eldritch power was needed. I experimented for a time. At great cost to two friends, I successfully created one daughter. Yet her fate was doomed." *My dear Maeve, may your soul rest peacefully in the bogs.*

He put the ax down. "You will learn to adore her beauty, for you are all modeled after her image. Alas, she is lost to us, and you will have different names and souls. See, the arts have recently been shown to me in the battlefield by the hybrid Empress, her actions revealed how to turn earth into flesh. She also left these four homunculi, rich with power. With Lysis abroad, I have been free to experiment with geomancy. To turn golems into beings with flesh and beating hearts."

He kneeled and they embraced him. The three instinctively touched their own arms as they wrapped about themselves. They compared it to the Doctor's; flesh was warmer. They were just beginning to understand what they were.

"The Rule of Independence is infused in your blood. You control your own heart. You will need names, so think upon who you are and how you want to be called."

The daughters listened. Three heads turned sideways, comprehendingly.

"Daughters, there is no need to choose names now. You have plenty of time for that. You have given your father hope. For with you, I have confirmed that I can create. And I have one more heart, a replacement for me, so I can become like you: independent. I shall turn my clay into flesh, and free myself from the blood bond of Lysis."

The last homunculus seeped in a bowl. Grave took *Hewnmaw* and laid it on the operating table beside it. He took off his apron. Aligning the scar on his chest with the blade, he pressed down his body. The scar split. Lysis' white blood streamed forth, as he pulled the chest open with his left hand. With his right hand, he grabbed the freshly prepared homunculus and inserted it…

THE ILL AGE

THE FATE OF Helen, Ruhyn, Servandum and Lysis will be revealed in the next installment of *Dyscrasia Fiction™ (coming soon, from IGNIS Publishing)*. Meanwhile, mature readers can read the legend of the Ill Age! Discover how Lord Lysis rose to power and conquered dyscrasia in *Lords of Dyscrasia (2011)*. Available from online retailers around the globe.

5/5 Stars "...there are few, if any, novels comparable to [*Lords of Dyscrasia*]...The pace is nearly breathless...makes the majority of current popular fantasy fiction read like recipes by comparison...highly recommended, though not for the faint of heart." - *ForeWord Clarion Reviews*

LORDS OF DYSCRASIA

A DYSCRASIA FICTION™ NOVEL

GRAPHIC SWORD & SORCERY
S. E. LINDBERG

About the Author & Dyscrasia Fiction

S.E. Lindberg resides near Cincinnati, Ohio working as a microscopist, employing his skills as a scientist and artist to understand the manufacturing of products analogous to medieval paints. Two decades of practicing chemistry, combined with a passion for the Sword & Sorcery genre, spurred him to write graphic adventure fictionalizing the alchemical humors. Connect with him *via his blog* or the Sword & Sorcery group which he *co-moderates on Goodreads.com.*

Dyscrasia Fiction™ explores the choices humans and their gods make as a disease corrupts their souls, shared blood, and creative energies. Historically, dyscrasia referred to any imbalance of the four medicinal humors professed by the ancient Greeks to sustain life (phlegm, blood, black & yellow bile). Artisans, anatomists, and chemists of the Renaissance evolved humorism to include aspects of alchemical elements (water, air, earth, and fire) and psychological temperaments (phlegmatic, sanguine, melancholic, and choleric). In short, the humors are mystical media of color, energy, and emotion; *Dyscrasia Fiction™* presents them as spiritual muses for artisans, sources of magical power, and contagions of a deadly disease.

GLOSSARY

Aleece	Bryhan's mother, whose soul is attached to the spear he carries
Arenites	Striped sandstone mountains used by Clan Tonn for colored glass; red is mercury oxide, orange is iron oxide, green and blues are other silicates and oxides
Behemoth	See "Centimani"
Bryhan, Guard	Lone possessed warrior serving Echo, once a royal Son from Clan Tonn
Calx mountains	Limestone range around Clan Tonn
Centimani	Many-bodied golem made of flesh from a variety of Spawnen and homunculi; a.k.a. "Behemoth"
Chepri	Ant-headed humanoids
Chromanti	The insectan-human hybrids; the chepri, the ant-headed humans
Chromlechon	The once-Queen's mountain colony, now used as a keep
Commons	City Tonn center, an amphitheater carved from an exhausted limestone quarry
Curators	Humans who heal and provide fuel for the Gray Lords via their banners or the Pyre

Dyscrasia   An imbalanced mixture; a fatal blood disease shared amongst elders and man that mutates victims

Echo, Foundling   A Gray Lord who seeks a purpose, a hybrid amongst humans

Elders   Ancient god-like creatures, including golem, insect, and avian kind

Empress   See "Veneda"

Eucrasia   A harmonious mixture; eucrasiac blood is *lapis elixir*

Ferrus Eviscamir   Lysis' Sword marked with Grave's failed promise, *"Queen, with this I will heal you"*

Ferrus   Grave's Ax inscribed with the promise:
Hewnmaw   *"Children, may this blade carve you life"*

Gorgepath   Valley trade route, once connecting Tonn to Qual to Lysis

Grave, Doctor   An earth golem, after serving the Once-Queen he was possessed by Lysis

Gray Era   Time period following the Ill Age in which the Gray Lords rule the Land

Gray Horde   Select prey of Lysis that are possessed by his blood; they are stationed in the Gray Orchard when not hunting with him

Gray Lords   Echo and Lysis; sorcerers who drain energy from art and beings, rendering them gray

Gray Orchard	A zone of crucifixes and poles around the Chromlechon Bogs that is populated by Lysis' carcasses (unpossessed dead) and his Gray Horde (reanimated soldiers)
Grotto Folk	Keeper type, live in caves on the exterior of the Chromlechon; harvest papyrus and create paper for curators
Harpies	The avian-human hybrids with human torsos and bird legs and wings
Hearth	See "Tonn Tomb"
Hollows	Secluded vault of the once-Queen in the Underworld (beneath the Chromlechon); birthplace of her golems including Grave
Homunculi	Dried fruit from the Ill Orchard; the seeds appear as miniature simulacra of Spawnen, and can be used as hearts for golems
Ill Age	The time in which mixing of blood and energy corrupted human and eldritch kind in the Land (preceding this book). The end of the Ill Age is marked with Lord Lysis' rise to power (chronicled in the novel Lords of Dyscrasia)
Ill Orchard	A mysterious tree in the land which the Empress originates; the source of dyscrasia
Keepers	Human refuges living in the Chromlechon

Land	The surface of the earth, a realm dominated by humans
Lapis elixir	The eucrasaic, white blood of the Gray Lords
Lapisplasm	Stone turned to living flesh by geomancy
Larvalwyrmen	Ancient larvae of the once-Queen, cursed never to mature upon her death, reanimated by Lysis
Lord Lysis	Gray Lord, protector of the humans who survived the Ill Age
Maeve, Lady	Lord Lysis' wife, Doctor Grave's sole daughter who died during the Ill Age
Melancholy	The alchemical humor (liquid) of the bogs
Once-Queen	The defeated, and reanimated, eldritch ant
Picti	Clan from which Lord Lysis hailed
Pyre	Lord Lysis' magical fire that transmutes creative energy into fuel for his white blood; also the source of his animated paper sprites
Qual, Clan	Weavers, dyers, thread makers; the clan with which Helen was most closely associated
Red Caps	The youngest of Keepers
Ruhyn, Master	Outsider from Clan Tonn, motivated to revitalize the City and bring joy back to the land

Rule of Animating the Dead	One of Doctor Grave's Arcane Axioms: "Possess the blood of a corpse to regulate its body; control its heart to direct its mind"
Rule of Blood and Ether	One of Doctor Grave's Arcane Axioms: "Blood is the medium bridging the physical world with the ethereal, connecting soul to body"
Rule of Matching Hue	One of Doctor Grave's Arcane Axioms: "The souls of the healthy living exhibit the same color in the astral realm as their oxygen-enriched blood does in the corporeal realm; mismatched hues indicate departure from homeostasis: illness"
Rule of Muses	One of Doctor Grave's Arcane Axioms: "Artists are inspired by the emotive ether, as they craft, they consume that which ignited their creativity"
Rule of Relics	One of Doctor Grave's Arcane Axioms: "Souls remain attached to their master's bones; emotions of artists remain with their art; memories adhere to their place of origin"
Rule of Sight	One of Doctor Grave's Arcane Axioms: "Ethereal memories, emotions, and souls remain invisible to those who see the physical world in color; those who *can see* the colors of ether, see the tangible world in gray"

Rule of Stone	One of Doctor Grave's Arcane Axioms: "Hybrid blood always calcifies: dyscrasiac (diseased) blood petrifies to solid limestone; eucrasaic (healthy) blood condenses to liquid stone, *lapis elixir*"
Servandum	The Gray Foundling's final imago, last in the Echo sequence
Sky	The air above the Land, a realm once ruled by the Avian King
Soldiers	Giant eldritch ants with elephantine tusks, possessed by Lord Lysis
Spawnen	Name used by the Empress that refers to anything red-blooded which emerges from the Ill Orchard, including humans (dryads), eldritch ants, or avian rocs
Sprites	Animated paper minions who communicate and scout on behalf of Lysis; formed in his Pyre
Sylphin	Horse sized, insectan-avian hybrid; cousin to the griffin
Theater	Doctor Grave's Lyceum, amphitheater for learning inside the Chromlechon Keep
Tonn Tomb	Sacred Hearth Monument, housing the glass sarcophagi under Tonn City
Tonn, Clan	Artisans of the earth, employing furnaces to manipulate metal, stone, and glass

Underworld	The realm under the Land, once ruled by the insectan Queen
Veneda, Empress	The Empresses invading the Land; a geomancer able to turn inanimate earth into living flesh
Wyverns	White-scaled serpents that feed on blood